The Hunting Party

NICOLE M. TAYLOR

EPIC
Press

The Hunting Party
Killers

Written by Nicole M. Taylor

Copyright © 2017 by Abdo Consulting Group, Inc.

Published by EPIC Press™
PO Box 398166
Minneapolis, MN 55439

Printed in the United States of America.

Cover design by Christina Doffing
Images for cover art obtained from iStockPhoto.com
Edited by Jennifer Skogen

LIBRARY OF CONGRESS CATALOGING-IN-PUBLICATION DATA

Names: Taylor, Nicole M., author.
Title: The hunting party / by Nicole M. Taylor.
Description: Minneapolis, MN : EPIC Press, 2017. | Series: Killers
Summary: When a "family" of murderous thieves is exposed and goes on the run across the
    Kansas prairie, earnest young Lawce Gibbon is pressed into service as part of an aggressive
    "hunting party" determined to track the murderers down.
 Identifiers: LCCN 2016946204 | ISBN 9781680764864 (lib. bdg.) |
    ISBN 9781680765427 (ebook)
Subjects: LCSH: Thieves—Fiction. | Murderers—Fiction. | Murder—Investigation—Fiction. |
    Mystery and detective stories—Fiction. | Young adult fiction.
Classification: DDC [Fic]—dc23
LC record available at http://lccn.loc.gov/2016946204

EPICPRESS.COM

For Lorrie and Rodney Taylor
with so much thanks for your
unstinting love and support

1

An Important Man

Emmelene Drake
Madalane, Kansas
December, 1871

The traveler must have been something special indeed. Byron ran into the house to report before he'd even stabled the horses and examined the man's vehicle. Byron was breathless, his cheeks scraped red from the bitter cold. He looked so young, all fat rosy cheeks and blonde curls. "He's a doctor," Byron told me, "from back East. The gig looks brand new and he gave me this." He held out his open palm with a gold dollar in it. I reached out to touch it and found it still cold.

All at once, I felt my tongue grow thick and arid. "Get him inside," I croaked. We would need to move fast; a well-heeled man in a good little buggy with dollar coins to throw around would never stay in a hovel like ours—that was, if we gave him a choice.

Byron nodded and vanished again out the door. He allowed it to slam helplessly behind him, which he always did, no matter how many times I had asked him to shut it nicely. The door was thin and cheap, like everything else we had, and we needed it to last through at least one more winter.

When I first came to this country, I imagined—I hoped—that I would never see a winter again, not like in my homeland. But I was very young then.

I smoothed out my skirt and breathed through my nose, reminding myself: this was good news, but not ideal. We didn't usually take our "one-way guests" this late in the season. Only an idiot would head out on the trail with winter looming on the horizon, especially with only a small, light buggy like a gig. Likely, this doctor was headed somewhere close by. Perhaps he had even thought to settle in nearby Madalane.

We always preferred those folks who had set their eyes on the golden country: Oregon or California. Those folks were intending to vanish. The people who loved them might not expect word for months or years.

While Byron was fetching the man, I hurried about making the place ready for him. It didn't take long. Our little cabin—built by Fader's inexpert hands—was home to us, inn to travelers, and even contained our small inventory of goods that folks needed if they were heading west. By dint of simple necessity, every single thing we had occupied its own niche.

I pulled the stretched hide off the top of the big wooden wardrobe that was Mamma's prized possession and spread it right in front of the door, like a rug. If the doctor looked close at it, he would see the dark stains that never seemed to scrub out. But they never looked close.

"Fader," I called out, "we have need of your hammer!"

. . .

I was right, of course. I saw it in the man's eyes as soon as Byron led him through the door. He saw our wattle and daub walls where the wind whistled through, and the big bed in the corner, a soiled nest for the four of us. He took in the dented tin plates and the poorly tended fireplace, oozing smoke throughout the room and casting everything in a dirty blue haze. Seeing exactly what we were, he wanted none of it; but before he could open his mouth to speak, Fader was already behind him. His aim was true, though he had been in his cups as usual, and he brought down the big blunt-headed hammer on the man's skull with all of his power.

It made the same sound it always did: a hard, damp slapping sound, like striking wet laundry on a rock. It was so simple. Just that one movement of Fader's arm and that unremarkable sound and the strange tense eagerness left the air, as though each one of us were slowly deflating.

The man crumpled onto the animal hide, scalp oozing slow, black blood. Mamma and I rushed forward to lift the corners of the hide into a kind of sling to move the body before the blood could penetrate to the wooden floor underneath.

"Take the body out and bury it," I told Byron. "Bury it deep this time or the next grave you dig will be your own." I flicked his nose as I said it but I was serious. Byron had been getting awfully lazy; just a few weeks ago when we got all the rain, that farmhand from New York had emerged from the earth like a bad memory. First the tips of his rotted toes came up, then the shining pate of his skull, picked clean by the worms and the beetles. Mamma and I had to rebury him quickly in the full afternoon sunlight when anyone might have passed by and seen us at our work.

The ground wasn't even hard yet, so Byron didn't have an excuse for his sloth.

"And hide the gig," I called after him. "We can strip it in the stables." The fewer people who saw it sitting unattended in front of our place the better. With a local, we ran an extra risk of encountering someone who might know—have known—the man and would recognize his brand new vehicle.

Fader stood in the door, his hammer hanging from one hand. A bit of hair and flesh was crusted on the end with only a little blood, though enough to drip on the floor. Mamma stepped forward and lifted it lightly from his fingers, taking it outside to scrape it off in the hard, scabby snow.

"He's a doctor," I told Fader, who nodded, glass-eyed from drink. "Probably looking to settle around here. Probably carrying everything he has in the world." I patted him on the shoulder and found his muscles there still tense, as though he were a dog on alert.

"*Viktig* man," he muttered. *Important man.*

"No more than any of the rest of them. Just richer."

Byron burst through the door again and I was about to shout at him for slamming it when I looked at his face. There was no color in his cheeks. "Em," he said. "There's a problem."

•   •   •

There was a part of me that wanted immediately to blame Byron. "You should have looked closer," I wanted to shout. I wanted to pepper him with slaps. But the truth was, it was I who had hurried him.

Before, we almost always sat with our one-way guests, fed them dinner and listened to their stories, oftentimes for hours. It gave Byron a chance to root through their things and decide if the bounty was worth the risk, but it also allowed us to feel a bit, well, *civilized*. We learned about our travelers, their burdens and their goals—Mamma called it our Last Supper. If we had taken the time to learn anything about our doctor from the east, we would have known that he was not traveling alone.

He had wrapped the little girl in blankets and furs, practically burying her on the soft leather seat.

As he had undoubtedly intended, the girl was in a deep sleep. She knew nothing of the stop her father had made, nothing of us or the inn.

"What shall we do?" Byron whispered, though if the babe had not been roused by any of the other commotion, I hardly thought that speaking at full volume would do it.

It was an idiot's question and Byron knew it. "What shall we do?" What was there to do? Take her into our house and pretend she was our own long-lost little one? She looked to be at least three or four, much too old to be a natural-born infant. There was only one thing to do and Byron had known it the moment he set eyes on the child.

"It's woman's work," he said stiffly. "Besides, I have him to deal with." He pointed his toe at the doctor from back east, half-covered by the tarp and lying on the cold ground between us. "He still needs work, I saw his chest move."

I would estimate that Fader's hammer did the job completely about two in three times. The third time, Byron had to finish Fader's work, usually with a hunting knife.

I heaved a great sigh and waved a hand at Byron, dismissing him. He grabbed the ends of the doctor's tarp with far more enthusiasm than usual and began pulling the dead man backwards toward the orchard and his eternal rest.

"Woman's work." It seemed there was no end to that. I stood on the long runner of the buggy, leaning over the sleeping child. She was a good-looking little girl: very long eyelashes, cheeks still plump with baby-fat, and wild brown curls sticking out from her hood.

That hood was impressive: a very vibrant cobalt blue, with fine embroidery all around its edge, little yellow and white wildflowers, so this girl would remember spring even in the cold of winter. Surely this child had been cherished and beloved since the day she slid screaming into the world. Surely she had been given every consideration, every comfort, every nourishment. Surely things would change considerably for her if she survived her father. A little girl needs her father, she needs her protector.

The cold made opaque clouds out of her breath. They issued from her pink mouth at regular intervals, but she did not appear to feel the chill. For her, right now, it was warm and safe, and she was on her way to somewhere new with her father who loved her.

If I acted quickly, I could make sure that—for her—that would always be true.

I did not require a hammer or a hunting knife; I did not require anything more than my own two hands. I used one hand to squeeze her nostrils closed and pressed the meat of my hand over her mouth so it could not gasp for breath. With my other hand, I held the back of her skull tightly so she could not wriggle away from me.

If her eyes fluttered open, if she saw me and was afraid, if she made a small sound deep in her throat, none of it mattered. A short, happy life was a gift most people weren't lucky enough to receive.

I held her in that fashion for several minutes. Longer, perhaps, than I needed to, but I wanted to be sure. When I was certain the little one was gone, I disentangled her from the blankets and lifted her into my arms. She was so much heavier, somehow, than a living child. Gently, I pulled the leather boots off her feet and the little blue cap as well.

Thus shorn, I delivered the child to the orchard, where it had begun to snow upon Byron and his unfinished task. He had the beginnings of a grave carved out from the earth, while the doctor lay next to him, a second red grin opened in his neck. I laid the little girl on her father's chest and tucked the hide around the both of them.

"Bury them together," I told Byron. "And hurry before they freeze solid."

2

Chivaree

Lawce Gibbon
Madalane, Kansas
December, 1871

Lena Klein—one of the Germans—had married again. I heard all about it from Mrs. George Burke, who was not at all pleased with the situation. If Pap charged people for standing around and running their mouths, our general store would be even more successful.

"Her man has been dead six weeks," Mrs. George Burke told me. "In the ground six weeks, ain't even had time to get cold. And here she is taking up with a new one."

The Germans weren't really German—not all of them at least. A couple families were Dutch; one man came from Sweden; some folks kept so much to themselves that none of us could say where exactly they hailed from. But they had all come to Madalane about the same time and settled in a little cluster on the north end of town, so we thought of them as all of a piece.

Lena Klein's dead husband, Henry, hadn't been German at all. He was a taciturn Northerner who shared no language but silence with his young bride. Neither of them had been much for socializing but everyone said that Henry was a fine drover, and we had mourned for him properly.

Lena apparently hadn't, at least as far as Mrs. George Burke was concerned. "It's greed, pure and simple. Gobbling up dessert before the dinner dishes is cleared."

It was not Lena Klein's supposed greed that galled Mrs. George Burke as much as it was the incredible ease with which she had secured a second husband, so hot upon the heels of the first.

Lena Klein could have herself two men inside

of two months because her hair was still black and glossy and her bosom still pointed straight ahead, unlike Mrs. George Burke's which looked gloomily toward the earth. Even when she'd had the advantage of a youthful glow, however, Mrs. George Burke had probably never been much of a looker. She had a propensity toward flat, black moles and they peppered her neck and face like flyspeck. She had done just about as well as she might have expected with George Burke, a shiftless sort who had come west because he couldn't manage to keep a job out east.

"And that boy she married!" Mrs. George Burke continued, seemingly unaware that I had yet to utter a single word. "Harris Parsons is little more than a kiddie! He should be looking to gals his own age."

Harris Parsons was indeed my own age, near seventeen. We used to go to school together, though he had dropped out two years ago to manage his father's farm. He was an only son.

It was true that Lena Klein was not exactly the

sort of woman I'd have expected him to take to wife. I would have ranked her in the third tier of marriageable women in town because of her age and her being married once before. Some folks said she had gotten with child once years ago and had lost it. That portended a weak womb that could not properly knit together the babe. With the solidity of a modest but profitable farm at his back, Harris could have indeed gotten a much better bride.

"Young folks." Mrs. George Burke shook her head at me, as though I had personally brokered the marriage between Lena Klein and her new paramour.

"Ma'am," I asked finally, "is there anything I can get for you?"

She looked slightly stricken, conscious that she was standing in a sundries store. "Ah. Yes. I needed some of your sprigged muslin, if you please."

"Of course. Charlie!"

Right away my brother emerged from the storeroom with a roll of muslin in his arms. I wondered if he had been listening covertly behind the store room door, just waiting for a chance to insert himself into the conversation.

"Making something new for little Mary, Mrs. Burke?" he asked, lips drawn back in an obsequious smile.

Charlie and I looked a lot alike—the same fluttery, haystack hair and brown eyes—but he did not suffer from freckles as I did, and his teeth likewise were very fine and straight while mine crowded my mouth like impatient children. I sometimes thought that we looked like two versions of the same item, Charlie having been produced after the craftsman had perfected his design.

Mrs. George Burke smiled to see Charlie, as women nearly always did. "Yes," she said, "I am indeed. She's outgrowing all of her things from last year. I swear, she is going to be as tall as her father."

"And as handsome as her mother!"

Charlie was clever, saying "handsome" instead

of beautiful. A truly plain woman—as Mrs. George Burke was—knows when she is being patronized. She knows that no one would call her beautiful, but she might flatter herself to imagine that someone could think her handsome.

"Charlie Blake," she said, as though his name itself were sufficient admonishment, but we had both seen the way she glanced down and allowed a pinkish blush to rise in her face.

"Is there anything else I can get for you? Some of that penny candy Mary likes?"

"Oh, I believe she's much too old for that. Young ladies shouldn't suckle on sweets like babes in arms."

Charlie made some approving noise and began to unfurl the bolt of muslin for Mrs. George Burke's inspection. "There's still some stock to be unloaded in the back," he spoke to me out of the side of his mouth as he would to any subordinate making a nuisance of himself. I retreated, however, because I did not want to get into another argument and certainly not in front of a paying customer. Besides,

Charlie had a way of twisting things in the recounting—even when I won, I still lost.

According to our father, we were both to "share" the managing of the store when he was not available. In practice, it was a constant power struggle, every task a fresh battle between the two of us. Points were scored for each customer who left with bulging packages and subtracted for every minute and hour of grunt work one was forced to do. Each of us kept a silent tally in our heads and the tallies rarely agreed. By rights, Mrs. George Burke should have been a point in my favor, but I knew that Charlie would count her for himself.

I stalked back to the storeroom, determined to leave it spotless and sparkling. Not that it would matter to our father. One good sale was worth a thousand shelves of painstakingly arranged stock.

Charlie was not my full-blood brother. He was the only fruit of a shameful moral lapse on our father's part shortly before he married my mother. Charlie was born six months before me, but we were nearly three years old before our father informed my mother that he had another child. In all the world, there can be no woman more singularly committed to the ideals of Christian charity than my mother because, when she heard this shocking news, her response was to insist that we bring the boy into our own household.

Some years later, she told me that she imagined that I, being so young, would grow to have no memory of the unnatural way Charlie had joined our family. She was wrong. I remembered clearly being my parents' only beloved child and, just as clearly, I remember when Charlie was introduced into the home. It felt like we were two horses squeezed into a pen made for just one.

Charlie was the worst sort of person: the sort who demands more than his share until he's left just scraps for everyone else. One would think that given a choice between two sons, one legitimate and one illegitimate, it would be an easy piece of work to divvy up a business. Charlie doesn't see it that way, though. As far as he is concerned, he is entitled to everything that I am and more if he can get it. I take comfort in one thing, however: even after all these years, Pap still hasn't given Charlie his name.

"We are to have a high time tonight!" Charlie burst through the storeroom door so effusively that he nearly toppled into me.

"Oh?"

Charlie crunched something loudly in his teeth. Penny candy. Pap didn't like it when we ate stock, which was why Charlie never did it when Pap was around. "We're going to give your friend and his German a good scare."

"Are we now?"

"Haven't you heard? We're getting up folks for a chivaree tonight. Gonna make some noise outside their place, keep 'em from having too good a time, eh?"

That sounded like a spectacularly bad idea. I knew little of Lena Klein but she had always struck me as a serious woman, unlikely to tolerate silliness or pranking. Harris I knew to be stalwart and a little dull. I'd never seen him participate in a joke, possibly because he rarely understood them. Neither of them seemed like the sort of folk who would appreciate Charlie and the hooligans he ran with disturbing their peace.

"Sounds like a waste of time to me," I told him. "It's not even their wedding night. Mrs. George Burke said they'd been married almost a week."

Charlie sat down on one of the wooden crates and drew his feet up underneath him. He would never have dared to do that in front of my father, acting like every damn thing he saw belonged to him. He was only like this when there was no one around to see him. No one but me.

"Oh, don't be so sour. It'll be a bit of fun, like a thief wallop." Whenever Charlie caught thieves—usually luckless kids not much younger than us—taking items from the store, he threw them out with an extra boot in their backsides. He called it a thief wallop.

"I got little interest in such things." Charlie could cleave to his boorish buddies if he demanded a companion. "Does Pap know what you're planning to do?"

Charlie laughed, showing all his fine, straight teeth. "Pap? Who d'ya think is organizing the whole thing?"

*   *   *

I had been to just one chivaree before, years ago when a young man and a woman in a wagon train had fallen in love during the journey from New York. I think the girl's parents organized the chivaree; they were something foreign, perhaps French? By the time I joined up with my mother and father, it was a great laughing mass of people, clanging pot lids and whooping and hollering like wild Indians.

We wound all the way through town like a parade and out to where the wagon train had settled. Folks had come together and put up one particular wagon for the new couple to share and they'd draped a blanket over the opening in the wagon bow for privacy.

As we encircled the wagons, someone started singing in a language I did not know. Others clapped and whistled or shook huge horse bells into the wind. We watched as shadows moved inside the canvas of the wagon. Being ten and small for my age, it was easy for the crowd to push me up close against the wagon. I could see the gal's face in profile, her sharp nose and slightly witchy chin.

The man emerged from the tent flap, just his head and his upper body. The woman lingered inside the tent; we could all see her shadow crouching next to him. He shouted something to the crowd, though I can't remember what in particular he said, and then he vanished again inside the wagon. When he emerged, he had his bride's head in his hands and covered her face with kisses. She didn't look much older than me and she was so red; I'd wondered if her skin burned his mouth.

That was my memory of what a chivaree was: a great laughing demand, satisfied by a gesture of love. I did not imagine that what Charlie and his friends had in mind would be in any way similar.

We gathered in front of Milt Johnson's house, in what could reasonably be called the "outskirts" of Madalane, a place where the houses grew sparser and sparser until they vanished into prairie grass and the occasional rough homestead. There were more folks than I had expected—some thirty or forty—and nearly all of them men.

I did spot a few wives—Mrs. Clare MacDonald and Mrs. Jack Husted amongst them—but they stood off to one side with an awkwardness about them, as though they had realized too late that this was not an occasion for them. The other chivaree had been lousy with women, waving homemade ribbons stuck all over with little metal and ceramic noisemakers, and children screeching along with everyone else. There was no one here under the age of fourteen or so.

Charlie was in the thick of things as usual. He had taken a big metal washtub from somewhere, probably right off someone's front porch, and he had a heavy metal spoon to knock around the inside. Occasionally, he would let out an awful sound, a little like a yowl and a little like a yodel. It reminded me of the sounds of the coyotes alerting one another in the hills at night.

I also spotted Katie Conkle in the crowd, hanging on to the edge of her father's waistcoat with one hand. That, at least, made me a bit glad that I had come. By any reasonable measure, Katie was the most eligible woman in town. She was almost exactly one year younger than me and her father owned the Empress Hotel, the most successful business in town—next to my father's store, of course. She was Abner Conkle's only child and his greatest comfort since his wife died some years ago. Whoever married her would surely inherit not only his business but also his contacts and supply lines. To any thinking person, it would only make sense that the

Conkle and Gibbon families should be joined to enhance the reach and efficacy of both businesses.

Besides her considerable dowry, though, Katie was also a thoroughly pleasant girl with an agreeable face and figure. That last bit was important because a very beautiful woman would never make a good wife. Foolish men had a bad habit of believing that a beautiful woman must also be a good one, a talented one, a smart one, and they would have told her so all her life. Nothing ruins a girl's character quicker or more completely than unwarranted compliments. You would never catch me chasing after some silly, spoiled beauty like Elize Wagner, Maggie Stearns, or any of the other girls that Charlie courted with such greasy ardor.

No, it was far better that a girl be healthy and hard-working, polite and serious. That was the sort of bride that would please Pap mightily, and Katie was all of those things. I had attempted to make my regard for her plain, but she was a great one for keeping her thoughts to herself. I tried to catch her eye through the milling crowd, but she wasn't paying any attention. Instead, she was looking out toward the Germans' homesteads with her eyebrows drawn together thoughtfully.

Someone in the crowd had started passing around a mysterious clay jug, undoubtedly full of liquor. When it reached me, I gave it a sniff to make sure and passed it to the next man, who drank from it as though it contained mother's milk. As the sun began to sink, it seemed to me that the shouts and cries were growing ever louder, but still the crowd waited, no one making a move out toward the low hills where Lena Klein had her cabin—until my father appeared, trotting gently down the road toward us with a smile on his face.

"Sorry, sorry!" he called, waving to us all. The crowd made a great roar of approval at the sound of his voice. Abner Conkle (who had availed himself of the clay jug) slapped him on the back wildly. Charlie, of course, rushed right over to him to show off his likely purloined tub and spoon. I kept a respectful distance and waited for Pap to speak.

"Alright," he said, pointing toward the Germans' homesteads. "Get at 'em!"

. . .

Someone pressed something into my hands—a ragged length of wood without any adornments or noisemakers. I accepted it more out of habit than desire, my fingers curling around it involuntarily.

I couldn't tell who had given me the stick; it was almost impossible to make out faces in the dark. A couple of men had thought to bring lanterns, and we followed their uncertain bobbing across the prairie. I only knew we had arrived at Lena Klein's cabin when the man in front of me stopped abruptly and I stumbled into him.

"Get around the side," someone hissed. "Surround the cabin."

Instead of making our presence clear with shouts and music, we moved, silent and dark, to swarm the little cabin. The men with the lanterns either doused them or tucked them inside their coats, leaving the rest of us to fumble in the darkness. It seemed that everyone but me had been issued instructions for this situation. I stretched out my arms until I felt the raw wood of the cabin with my fingertips. I pressed my shoulder against the wall and slowly made my way around the cabin until I bumped into a small, vaguely feminine figure.

"Katie?" I asked, for it was indeed Katie Conkle, clutching one of those half-dead lamps in her arms like an infant. The weak yellowish light made her only barely recognizable.

"Hey Lawce." Her eyebrows were still tight with worry.

"I thought all the women decided to stay back in town."

"Pa told me that a chivaree was like a celebration. A party."

"It is," I said immediately, but even in my own ears the words sounded doubtful.

Then, from the other side of the cabin, came a

series of whooping sounds, like wild men on the hunt. This must have been some sort of signal because out came the lanterns and what appeared to be a few torches as well, and it seemed like the whole prairie erupted in sound. The clanging of metal, the singing of bells, but mostly, overwhelmingly, the shouting of men.

Most of the shouts were wordless but, here and there, I could make out certain sentiments. "Come out," I heard more than once, along with "adultery" and even "murder!"

Katie and I remained silent, her lamp remained shielded, and we both pressed ourselves against the wall of the cabin. I imagined that I could hear movement inside, the sound of boots on wood or furniture creaking.

Someone had taken up the cry of "Come out! Come out! Come out and face us!" and some of the men had even gathered around the front door to pound it with their fists. A yellow light flared inside the cabin.

Light oozed out of the cabin in between the logs in front of us; the place had been poorly chinked and daubed, it seemed. Katie leaned forward and pressed her face against one small crack. "See anything?" I asked.

"Nothing much. Just shapes."

The knocking on the door had grown steadily louder, transforming from a few errant knocks into a barrage of blows. And then, abruptly, it stopped altogether.

I crept around the side of the cabin. Katie grabbed the edge of my jacket the way she had held on to her father's before. It felt strangely comforting, as though I were being tethered to something stolid and imperturbable.

When I poked my head around the corner of the cabin, I could see the open door clearly, a spill of light from the cabin illuminating Harris and the men crowded in front of him. Harris looked as though he had been roused from sleep with his britches hastily pulled on. He was still holding them up with one hand, the other hand poking an accusing finger at the crowd in front of him.

"Don't you fools have anything better to do than make trouble?"

It was, to my mind, an eminently reasonable question, but it only seemed to inflame the crowd further. Someone yelled something about him sleeping in a dead man's bed, and Harris set his mouth in a thin, unfeeling line. "My bed is no business of yours!"

I heard someone yelling then, something about his "German whore," and I don't know who made the first move. It would not have been entirely unlike Harris to take a swing at an aggressor—he had never been one to tolerate bullies—but it might have just as easily been some stumbling drunk trying to snatch him out of the house.

Either way, an all-out scuffle was soon underway in the open door of the cabin. I heard rapid footsteps inside as Harris was forcibly dragged away from the light of the cabin and out toward the darkness where the rest of the men were waiting.

As Harris struggled in their grasp, he lost his grip on his belt and his pants fell, pooling around his ankles and tripping him up. There was something terrible and pathetic about Harris, naked in the torchlight, struggling to cover himself while the men held his arms.

It seemed that they found something pitiful in it as well, the kind of wretchedness that inspires rage instead of tenderness. Someone started kicking him and it wasn't long before the others joined in, a big tangle of limbs and fury and blows.

There were no bells now, no noisemakers. There were the occasional war whoops, though, and the dull sounds of flesh colliding with flesh. I saw, briefly silhouetted, someone with a stick like mine holding it over their head, bringing it down into the seething mass that had formed over Harris's prone body.

"They're gonna kill him," Katie said dully from somewhere behind me.

It felt suddenly as though I had been crouched

there alongside the cabin for a thousand years. My knees whined in protest, the tops of my legs were starting to freeze. I wanted to move, to run out there and do something. Say something. Throw myself into that dervish of human flesh and see what happened next.

But I could not will my body to move from where I crouched.

Before I could do anything—or even continue to do nothing—a great vibrating gunshot rang out. It rattled the dust from the cabin walls, which fell on Katie and me like the finest snow. Lena Klein had appeared in the door, an old Springfield rifle in her hands.

The crowd paused in its wild work to look at her, and she just stood there in her long white nightgown and her bare feet, black braid laid heavy over one shoulder. Her silence seemed to hold them all in a strange fairy-spell of stillness. It occurred to me that I had never heard Lena Klein utter a word of English beyond the occasional "yes" or "thank you." Close as

I was, I could see that she was trembling even as she held the gun on the men.

I was on my feet before I fully realized what I was doing. My legs had gotten so cold crouching there that it was like walking on pillars of air. I half floated over to the men, over to Harris who was lying at the center of them on the cold ground, smeared with mud and what was probably his own blood.

"Look at this," I said, loud and jovial, the same way I greeted customers in the store. "We got a sharpshooter amongst us! Harris, did you know when you wed her that you were getting such a fierce bride?"

I laughed heartily at my own joke as I bent down to help Harris to his feet. He was uncertain, leaning heavily on my shoulder. "Her house, her rules. Hell, even her gun. Don't you think this poor man has suffered enough?" I clapped Harris on the back. It was the wedding toast I'd never given him.

They weren't laughing with me, not yet, but some of that terrible energy had gone out of the air.

"Fellas, we ought to go home and thank our own wives for putting up with us without getting out the artillery!"

That got a few chuckles and I helped Harris over to the place where his pants had fallen. He pulled them on quickly, breaking away from my grasp like a petulant child eager to perform tasks on his own. "Say something," I muttered close to his ear. "Poke fun at yourself."

Harris gave me such a black look, I wasn't at all sure he was going to follow my advice. Then he flicked the band of his pants and said loudly, "Better get these britches back to her . . . "

The crowd erupted in laughter and something unwound inside of me. Harris used the opportunity to get back to the house, pushing Lena gently inside. At some point, Katie had made her way over from our hiding place. What just happened?" she asked me, gesturing toward the crowd of men, who were now carousing merrily off back in the direction of town.

"No one hates a poor dupe. No one gets jealous of a harridan."

Katie took this information in thoughtfully. Finally, she rested one of her little white hands on my shoulder. "That was a fine thing to do, Lawce."

I smiled at her, but weakly. I could see Pap and Charlie in the crowd heading back for town, Pap's arm slung comfortably around Charlie's shoulder.

3

Message From the Dead

Emmelene Drake
Madalane, Kansas
February, 1872

Americans are obsessed with the dead. I don't know if it is their recent war or some fundamental morbidity in the country's character, but if you proclaim yourself to have access to the spirit world, you will never go hungry in America. Mamma taught me that, but I quickly surpassed her in talent and popularity. Mamma is a sturdy woman with thick forearms and a strong back; she looks more like a laundress than a medium. I have cultivated a tendency toward slightness in myself. My eyes are big and look bigger with hollows underneath them. My bones are light and easily exposed at my wrists, my throat. My hair is long and fine and very pale. I look like a wisp of white smoke, like something seen only on the edges of one's vision.

In every city and territory where we have stayed, I have been able to open at least some small sideline in séances and spirits.

So I was not exactly surprised when the well-to-do woman appeared at my door, though I had posted no bills about an upcoming séance. I knew that she was well off from the little fox-fur muff she had tucked her hands into. I knew she was not from the plains because if she were, she would likely have selected gloves instead. Out here, even the richest amongst us have need of our hands.

"Welcome," I said when she appeared in the doorway. "We have a small array of traveling goods." I was careful not to mention the séances, though that was surely what this well-heeled woman desired. I prefer to let others (usually Mamma and Byron if he is around) speak for me on that score. It is preferable to play coy and mysterious, my "powers" a half-secret never uttered by my own lips.

The woman shook her head, all demure. She had bright black eyes and the sort of figure that would run to stoutness as she aged, but now, in the full bloom of her youth, she appeared pert and pleasantly chubby. It was easy to imagine her presiding over a grand table, graciously conversing with her honored guests.

She moved about the room slowly, reaching out occasionally to touch the rough homespun bags full of chicory and dry cornmeal. She paused in front of our long table, finally extracting her hands from the fox fur to tap a delicate fingernail on the tin plates.

"We serve dinner and supper and we have a room available for the night," I offered mildly, and she made an agreeable noise in her throat.

I wondered whom she had lost. A parent or a sibling? She struck me as young but certainly not too young to have a husband or children dead in the ground. When a woman came alone to me, it was very often to see a child, infants in particular. Something in men seemed to harden them against the death of a small child, maybe because a man must learn to love a child as it grows, while a woman's body gives her no choice but to develop some tender feeling before the little creature is fully formed.

"I heard some talk of you, Miss Emmelene Drake," the woman said, her back now to me as she examined our stingy little collection of cloth goods. "Folks say you are a medium of remarkable sensitivity."

I shook my head and made my face very grim. "I don't know about all that. But I am able to help some folks, from time to time." I paused for just a few moments before I added. "Are you in need of help?"

"I rather think I am." The woman turned around to reveal tears pressing perilously close to the edge of her eyes. In her hands, she was worrying a bit of blue fabric. It had been part of the little girl's winter hat. Mamma had broken it down into its individual parts, and we were selling it as a ready-made hat shape. Somehow, though, I did not like to see them in her hands. It made me feel something slow and cold in my stomach, as though icy water was slowly being dripped down inside me.

I could not say why, but suddenly I wanted to get this woman out of the cabin, to get her as far away from us as I could. "I'm sorry, I don't do manifestations for just one person. It's exhausting, you see, contacting the spirit realm—"

"But I'm not alone," the woman interrupted. The tears gave her eyes a strange and somewhat fearsome glitter. "My brother-in-law is with me and our hired man as well."

I leaned over to the window and drew our makeshift curtains to reveal Byron standing in the yard with a sepulchral older man in a very tall black hat. I could tell Byron was uncomfortable from the way he cracked his thumbs repetitively, staring down at his own hands and refusing to look directly at the man.

In their buggy—a little rented thing—I spotted a boy of fifteen or sixteen, but broad-shouldered nonetheless. As much as I misliked this water-eyed woman, I misliked the two men even more. They had a sense of waiting to them, like a pickpocket malingering in the street while his mark approached.

But I could not let fear master me. Instead, I forced myself to look closely at this unsettling scene, to really *think* about what I was seeing.

Something about how she worried at the blue hat was suggestive to me. She spoke as though she had hardened her heart against me, but her tears suggested that there was yet some womanly softness inside her; and what moved women better than the suffering of some dumb creature?

I reached my hand down to clutch at my lower belly and twisted my face in agony, letting out a grunt like a disagreeable milch cow. "I'm sorry, the child in my belly is twisted somehow. It is sure to be an awfully difficult birth." I waddled to

the table and sat down heavily, the woman looking at me with an uncertain expression on her
face.

I sucked breath through my teeth and shud-
dered slightly. I was hoping to produce a sheen of
sweat on my face. The woman's eyes flicked toward
the door as though she were thinking of running
out to the safety of her menfolk.

I grabbed her hand and pressed it against my
belly. "Here," I said. "Can you feel how he moves?"
Under her hand, I forced the flesh of my stomach
to quiver and agitate like a true unborn babe. "I am
seven months gone, but he is so small!"

I imagined how I must look to her: gaunt and
winter-white with this jolting creature in my flat
belly. Something like horror and something like pity
showed in her face. There, that was it.

"I'm sorry," I murmured, letting my head flop to
one side, "you wanted to talk to the spirits? Fader
says we need the money, so . . . "

"N-no," the woman stammered, pulling her hand

from my grasp. "No, you're unwell. Another day, I think."

I looked up at her through my eyelashes, as long and white as my hair. "Fader says the baby will be born dead like the others, but he fights so hard. I think he will live. Do you think so?"

The woman was backing away from me, the scrap of blue still enclosed tightly in her fist. "I don't know," she said. "I don't know at all. But you shouldn't . . . do this. It's not good for your health."

Comfortable and petted women always believed that human beings were so very fragile because they themselves had never been forced to discover just how much suffering a body can endure.

"Please, come back when I am better," I said in my weakest murmur. "Fader will whip me if he knows I turned away a paying customer."

When she closed the door behind her, I crept over to the window to watch her leave. She went to the tall man and muttered something in his ear, and the two of them exchanged looks of misgiving.

Byron, still standing before them, looked confused, but he was smart enough to keep his mouth closed. I taught him that.

Alone now in the cabin, that same cold trickling feeling resumed deep in my belly. Each freezing drop felt like a second ticked away on a clock. When Byron came in a few moments later, I was already pulling out the big chests Fader and I had brought all the way from Sweden.

"We have to leave this place," I told him.

4

Ride Out

Lawce Gibbon
Madalane, Kansas
February, 1872

The widow burst through the door in one great explosion of sound and winter cold and black silk poplin. She nearly ran up to the counter where Charlie was waiting, her skirts a dark, roiling cloud around her. Her hair had clearly been neatly arranged in one of those elaborate falls of curls that women favor nowadays, but the wind had blown strands of it free to coil wildly around her ghostly face.

"Are you a man of standing in this town?" she demanded.

"Well, I like to think I will be one day," Charlie

grinned. "Ma'am do you need some winter wear? Your poor hands look frozen." He reached out and covered her hands with his own, rubbing her bone-white skin vigorously.

I snorted loudly and leaned my broom against a barrel of flour. Charlie, that great defender of morality, was flirting outrageously with a woman in obvious widow's weeds.

"My brother and I are watching the store for our father," I told the woman. "Pap owns this place. *He* is a man of stature in Madalane."

It was true enough. Pap had come out here when it was still just tall grass and Indians and built one of the first supply outposts in Kansas territory. He was sixteen then, he liked to remind me. Just one year younger than myself.

"If you care about this place," the woman said severely, "if you don't want vile murderers in your midst, come to the courthouse in one hour." Her hand was still underneath Charlie's, but both of them seemed to have forgotten it there.

"What do you mean, ma'am?"

Come to the courthouse. One hour." She finally drew her hands away from his. "I must go. There are many others to warn."

"Poor addled thing," Charlie said as the widow struggled to close the door against the bitter wind.

"She's too rich to be addled." The rich did not let their mad folks run around in the street, and they certainly did not drape them in furs and expensive fabrics.

I moved back over to the flour barrel and retrieved my broom. "What are you doing?" Charlie asked me, though it should have been obvious.

"Waiting one hour," I said.

●　●　●

Our courthouse—which was also our jail and our meeting hall—was modest with only a small series of steps in front and a long wooden porch. By the time Charlie and I got there, the crowd had grown such that it was nearly impossible to see the little widow woman on the porch. Instead, we saw a tall black hat. Out of keeping, I thought, both for the season and occasion. The hat bobbed back and forth on the porch, its owner presumably making conversation with the people who had pushed to the front.

I spotted Abner Conkle and I wondered if Katie was in attendance. To my surprise, I also spotted Harris Parsons, the bruises on his face still a faint pond-scum green. I hadn't seen much of either of them since the chivaree, though Lena had come in once or twice to purchase goods. She did not acknowledge the thing we both knew had happened and instead looked at us the way she always had—as though we were no more interesting or intelligent than an unhewn block of wood.

Harris was talking to Mrs. Christopher Doubleday but I held the distinct feeling that he was very aware of my presence in the crowd and was intentionally avoiding my eyes. Well, that was his own lookout then.

"Hey," Charlie grasped my arm, "it's Pap!"

It was indeed. He was emerging from the court-house with the Sheriff Tomas Atkins to one side of him and my mother to the other.

"Even Georgiana is here." Even Charlie was not so bold as to address my mother by anything other than her Christian name.

"Folks," the sheriff said, cupping his hand around his mouth, "seems we've got a situation here."

"Sure as shit we do!" Pap added to a smattering of cheers from the crowd.

"C'mon," Charlie gave my shoulder a little shove, propelling me through the crush of people toward the front.

The top hat belonged to a very tall man with a grim face. He was looking back and forth between the sheriff and our father, with an unreadable expression on his face.

"Seems there've been reports of mischief outside of town."

"Mischief!" the widow woman rose up from the

bench. With her huge black skirts underneath her, she looked like a mermaid emerging from the darkest of seas. "My husband is dead! My child is gone!"

Her words sent an immediate thrill through the crowd. Folks began to mutter amongst themselves, began to shift from foot to foot just to have an excuse to move around.

"Ma'am, all respect to your grief," the sheriff began, "but there's no proof of that. People go missing on the trail—"

"My brother was not an irresponsible man," said the man with the top hat, "and he wasn't on the trail. He was looking to set up a practice here in Madalane. He had no quarrel with the Indians and did not engage in gambling or any other sort of low business. He had no reason to 'go missing' amongst you unless he met with villainy."

"Who done it?" a familiar voice from the crowd called out. I looked over my shoulder to see Harris standing on his toes to shout up at the assembled in front of the courthouse door.

Others in the crowd picked up his cry. "Who is it?" they shouted at the sheriff.

"We don't want to say anything before we've had a chance to get a proper look." The sheriff gave Pap a pleading look, and I saw Pap look briefly from him to Mama and back. Mama had put her hands on the widow's shoulders and drawn her lips almost entirely into her mouth, just leaving a hard white line in their place. Pap and I both knew what that meant.

"It was the Drakes," Pap said, even as the sheriff gave him a glare that could have felled a steer.

A great frustrated roar went up from the crowd. I would wager that there were not many in the crowd who were particularly surprised by this revelation. Even amongst the foreigners and outsiders, the Drakes were a species apart.

They eked out a wretched living just far enough from Madalane that folks heading for the trail would be tempted to buy their overpriced, half-rotted goods or stay in their straw-tick bed. They would even send the girl into town to entice travelers with promises of finer, cheaper rooms and a better selection of goods. Promises, of course, that they could not keep.

There were some young men who thought the daughter—Emmelene I remembered she was called—was very lovely and that was more or less true. It may have even been the reason the Drakes were able to lure anyone into their glorified shack. She would never, however, be a real marriage prospect for any man from a good family. Certainly not while she was offering those damned table-rapping sessions.

"Now, don't go tying yourself into knots." The sheriff sounded like a man trying to scoop spilled water back into a bucket with his hands.

From the back of the crowd, Harris's voice rose up again. "Call for a posse! Ride out!" Some folks even clapped for him.

"I'll ride out with you," Pap said immediately.

"We'll come too!" Charlie shouted.

I had gotten so caught up in the reaction of the

crowd that I had practically forgotten that Charlie was next to me. I wasn't sure whether I should be annoyed at him volunteering me without asking or relieved that he did not step up first, forcing me to do the same, lest I appear to be nothing but a follower.

"Goddammit Lawrence," the sheriff murmured to my father. If we had been farther away, we would not have heard it over the excited organizing of the crowd. "You better keep these boys in line because I sure as hell can't."

* * *

In the end, there were six of us: the sheriff, Pap, Charlie and me, Abner Conkle, Harris, and one of Charlie's friends, Patrick. Patrick was the fourth son of a farmer and built like one of his daddy's barns. A local man volunteered his fastest teams, and Mr. Stapleton offered use of his rental buggies and sledges. Those not chosen showed up at the store to offer us a motley assortment of weapons, old carbine rifles and brand-new pistols, and Charlie brought along his big hunting knife.

"You planning on skinning a deer out there?" I asked him.

"Might do. You never know what's going to happen on a hunting party."

He spoke as though he were intimately familiar with the particulars of such a thing. I wondered how he had developed that effortless sense of ease even in the most irregular situations.

But Charlie was more than just at ease; he was excited. This was a chance for him to excel—to prove that he was brave and strong and could dispense justice as needed. I could balance the store's books for a dozen years and not prove myself as indispensable as Charlie might on this one excursion.

It was that very thought that kept me from going to my father and begging to be removed from the posse.

"This belonged to my Delilah," the widow woman told my father and handed him a scrap of blue fabric with trembling hands. "I have little hope for Jonathan. He would have found me, were he still living. But Delilah was so . . . small. I should never have let them come alone. I should have come no matter what," her face folded in on itself, all aching regret.

"You were ill," her brother-in-law said, resting a hesitant hand on her shoulder. "You might have died yourself." It seemed to me that she would have preferred a wasting death on the trail to the constant misery she found herself in now.

She sniffed, drew herself up slightly, and addressed herself to Pap. "They might have spared her. There is a young woman with them. She is with child herself and she is afraid. I think she would have taken pity on my girl."

My father took the scrap of blue and the woman's hands as well. He stared into her face with the grave and intimate look that had made him one of the most trusted men in Madalane. "If she is to be found, I shall find her."

This was the first news I had heard of Emmelene Drake being in the family way. She had no husband and there was no one in town who would own to being a suitor of hers. A few possibilities presented themselves, each more unpleasant than the last. One thing was certain: any child born into that family would be unfortunate indeed.

"You boys ready yet?" the sheriff called wearily. "Gonna be full dark before we get there at this rate."

He was right, even with the fastest team in town, the Drake homestead was nearly sixteen miles from town. Would they be expecting us? Or would we come upon them like a surprise summer storm, rousing them from their beds as we had Harris and his new wife?

As we all hustled out to the waiting horses, I noticed that Katie Conkle had appeared amongst the crowd. Her face was heavy with anxiety, and she was carrying a small bundle wrapped in bright red fabric.

I expected her to approach her father, but when she saw me come out the shop's door, her eyes widened and she headed straight for me.

"You going with the men?" she asked me. It stung slightly, not being included with "the men," but I just nodded at her. "Well, take this then." She handled her little bundle to me. "It's not much," she admitted as I lifted the fabric to find a generous portion of roast beef neatly packed in paper and a chunk of brown bread. "But I thought you might get hungry."

"I hope our mission will be short," I told her.

"If you don't want it, I can—"

"No! No, that's not . . . no. I meant . . . just . . . thank you. This was very thoughtful of you."

Silence bloomed between us, and Katie licked her lips uncertainly. "It's good that you are going, Lawce. You can look after the rest of them."

"Clearly you have never seen me shoot."

Katie's mouth turned up a little at my meager joke. "That's not what I meant," she said. "You know what I mean."

I tucked her cold dinner into my pack along-side Pap's old Colt revolver that I dearly hoped never to touch. "I know," I said. "I will do my best." Katie Conkle gifted me one more of her smiles before taking her leave to tell her father goodbye.

I climbed up in a speedy little trap beside Charlie, who would drive the team. Next to me, he seemed almost to vibrate, one of his boots making a little scraping sound on the wood of the front board as he tapped it unceasingly.

From one of the single horses, Harris gave a sharp, high "whoop-whoop!" and Charlie answered him, flicking his whip over our team's back as he did so. We jolted into life, Charlie leaning into the drive with a laugh.

"Can you imagine," he asked, "the looks on their faces when we arrive?"

For Charlie at least, all of this would be a great joke.

"I can imagine," I told him.

•   •   •

It was noticeably colder sixteen miles out from Madalane, and I regretted not taking along any rugs or blankets to cover my legs. Though if I had, Charlie surely would have laughed at me for behaving like a delicate lady rather than a young man.

When Charlie said, "I see it ahead," it was the first he had spoken to me in nearly an hour.

I had only seen the Drakes' cabin once before, a few years ago when Pap went to have it out with Mr. Drake over an inventory problem. I never knew the particulars, but it seemed that some of Pap's stock wasn't making it to the store, and he had reason to believe that the Drakes had something to do with it.

Charlie, I realized, had not gone on that particular excursion and had likely never seen the Drake property. "That's their place," I assured him. "I remember the stable."

I had been suffused with pleasure at being asked to go along on Pap's business and largely concerned with making certain that I didn't do the wrong thing. I didn't dwell much on the Drakes themselves, except to register that they seemed just as odd as people said they were.

They had been new to Madalane then, and it would be a few weeks even before Emmelene started up her séance nonsense. It was she who dealt with Pap, translating Mr. Drake's high, fluting speech into English and Pap's into whatever it was they spoke. She struck me as shy and tender, and she certainly looked as though a strong breeze would blow her to pieces. It seemed a shame that she should be bound to this grim, joyless family in this hard and lonesome place.

Charlie and I were the first to arrive, though Pap and the others followed in short succession. The lights were all dark inside the house, and though they must have heard the horses approaching, no one appeared to greet us.

"They ran," the sheriff announced, pulling up in a buggy with Patrick and Pap.

Pap hopped down from the seat. "I told that woman I would find her daughter, or at least word of her."

Charlie, of course, leapt out of the buggy after Pap and I followed him at a more sedate pace. The rest of the men fanned out in different directions, some heading for the outbuildings, others for the orchard and paddock at the back of the house. Charlie and I went inside to join Pap.

The Drakes had gone, but I would wager that we had missed them by scant hours. The place had that smell to it, that moist, organic smell of too many bodies living too close up against one another. The coals banked in the fireplace still had some color to them, even. They were traveling light. Dishes were still in the cabinets, blankets on the bed. There were still big bags of cornmeal and flour, things I would have imagined they would have taken on a long journey, if only to sell off later.

Charlie was rooting through a small pile of ready-to-wear gear they'd set out while Pap was crouched down in front of the door, peering closely at the wood floor. I drifted toward the bed, the greasy covers still half-tangled, as though someone had just arisen. The bed was low-slung and made of straw-ticking that clearly no one had replaced in a long time. It was compressed into just a few flat inches. There was an unusual smell rising from the bed—more than just human dirt. There was something profane about it, like maggoty meat.

In the tiny space between the bed's mattress and the floor, someone had awkwardly tried to secret a rolled up piece of fabric or hide. As I crouched down to examine it, the rotten smell grew stronger.

I pulled it out with some difficulty. It was indeed hide and an old one to judge by the way the sewn edges were crumbling. I unrolled it on the wooden floor and was staggered by the reek. Across the room Charlie half-choked. I heard a heavy thunking sound as something enfolded in the hide dropped out and hit the floor hard.

"What the hell is that stink?" Charlie asked.

"A whole lot of blood," I said dully, getting to my feet.

Unrolled, the hide was about as long as a man was tall, and it was a fawn color, except in the places where black blood had soaked into the surface. The blood was raised in several places, as though it had thickened there, or else some other piece of bodily matter had been shed upon its surface.

Pap and Charlie approached slowly. "It smells like the Grim Reaper's own breath," Charlie murmured with uncharacteristic poetry.

"God is good." Pap's voice shook as he stared at the irregular pattern of black stains. Together, we looked at the horrible artifact for several long moments before Pap gestured to me. "Bring it out, show the others."

Halfway through my unpleasant task, I uncovered the source of the strange sound I had heard earlier: a large and brutal hammer. The handle was smooth from years of use and the head was oddly globular, as though it had been crafted by a none-too-skilled metal worker. When I picked it up, I discovered that it was heavier than a usual hammer as well. One end of the hammer's head was dulled and darkened, and I could guess at how that had happened.

I approached Pap wordlessly and handed him the awful thing. "Savages," he said.

Patrick and the brother were already waiting for us when we got outside. "I saw Jonathan's team in the paddock," he said. "Half-starved, but they're the same animals."

"Some manner of violence was done here," my father said, pointing toward the hide and the ground before us. "I'm sorry to say that I expect your brother has gone on to the next world." He let the hammer hang in one hand, its terrible misshapen head pointing toward the snowy ground.

The brother only nodded. I imagined that he had long ago come to the same conclusion and had accustomed his heart to the loss. Still, it could not have been easy to look upon a dirty hide, a rough-hewn hammer, the small and ugly way his brother had died.

Then, from around the edge of the cabin, Abner Conkle and the sheriff appeared. They wore identical blank expressions, and their faces had a strange dull pallor to them, like clothing left too long in the sun.

The sheriff cleared his throat, but when he did speak, he still sounded creaky and stiff. "Y'all better come around to the orchard."

Harris and Patrick brought along lanterns from the gigs and raised them aloft so we could see where we were setting feet as we made our way out into the orchard. It was snowing, soft and hazy, more like a thick fog than true snowflakes, and we saw almost immediately what the sheriff was talking about.

Underneath one of the apple trees with its grasping black branches, there was a raised hump of earth covered in a thin layer of snow. It was, unmistakably, a grave. As I looked, however, I slowly realized that it was not the only irregularity in the landscape.

One, two, three . . . the earth around the apple trees rolled and bucked like an unbroken horse.

In the summer when the grasses were high, it might have been impossible to distinguish, but now as winter had killed most everything, the full extent of the Drake family's depredations were as clear as the cold winter stars above.

"Boys," the sheriff said softly, "we have digging to do."

5

The Lemon House

Emmelene Drake
The Southwest
February, 1872

The wagon had belonged to a pair of adventurers, two young bucks so sure that there was a fortune waiting in the golden country and sure as well that they were the men to make it. We killed them as they slept because I was not at all certain that they couldn't overpower Fader and escape.

The furs in the back came from a trapper headed into Madalane to ply his wares. That had been a very happy accident indeed. We had never seen a fully loaded trapper come through, before or since. The pelts were indeed exceedingly warm.

We had other assorted goods that we could trade

or sell. All the sentimental trash that folk burden themselves with before the real hardship of the trail begins, the occasional gold tooth, rings and other jewelry. I confess myself partial to jewelry. It is an excellent way of consolidating value into something small and portable that can hide in plain sight. For some time, I had been wearing around my waist a pouch of such pieces, lifted from amongst the cache we kept in the cabin and sometimes taken from the bodies before Byron had a chance to go through all the pockets and bags.

I took no more than what might be considered my share. Less, in fact, considering all the work I did just in keeping us all alive and free. Were it up to Fader or Mamma or—heaven forbid—Byron, we would still be back in our little homestead waiting for the law in Madalane to string us up from the nearest tall tree.

And it was I, of course, who had discovered Nesbitt's Creek.

Our little wagon was shockingly fast, even

though the horses were skinny and the ground slick with snow. We reached Blossom Valley and its train station before nightfall, which gave us enough time to purchase two sets of tickets. For Fader and Mamma, a pair of tickets back east to Michigan, for Byron and myself, two passes to Texas.

Sitting in the station, Byron relentlessly tapped his feet against the floorboards, a homely little dance of his own devising. He kept looking at the doors as though expecting lawmen to burst in at any moment.

"Stop it," I said, digging my elbow into his side.

"They're gonna know."

I rested my hand on the cap of his knee and pressed it down until his foot flattened against the ground. "They are not going to know. Not until it's too late."

Mamma and Fader's train had left an hour earlier. By now they would be nearly to the next station where they would exit, hiking up the track a bit to await the train to Arizona. Byron and I would do the same when our train came, and when the law came here looking for us, they would look in Michigan and in Texas.

I had done such things before but I knew Byron had not. And so I tried to be gentle when I said, "Stop your shaking. You must help me with the henna and you're not allowed to make mistakes."

We would all have to change our appearance in some way. My hair took henna well and a different sort of wardrobe could do much to transform a woman. Fader would have to cut his beard and mustache and Mamma was to abandon her feigned Swedish accent and use her real voice. As for Byron, I was unsure. He had never been able to grow facial hair, just little golden patches on his cheeks. Perhaps his hair should be dyed as well, maybe black with bitter walnut dye?

Most folks took little notice of Byron, though. Even if they did, he had a way of sliding off their minds almost as soon as they took their leave of him.

It was an admirable and very useful quality; some might say that it was his one great talent.

"All right, Em," he said, placing his hand over mine and trying to smile. Byron was a good boy for all his flaws. An obedient boy.

"Remember to use my new name. I won't be Emmelene in Nesbitt's Creek."

He nodded fervently, his hand still clutching mine. Byron needed a lot of reassurance. At night, when we all curled into our shared bed, Byron used to loop his arms around my waist and press his face against my back like a child hiding from the thunder. He would hold me so tightly sometimes that I couldn't sleep. Instead, I would just lie there waiting through the night for the sun to rise and him to release me.

*   *   *

I met Byron in a train station very much like this one. I was thirteen, he was nine. He had a note he couldn't read pinned to his shirtfront, telling anyone who looked that he was headed for Mrs. Cynthia Rand's Whitewood Farm. That was also my destination, though I suspected we were going for very different reasons.

It was just Byron and me on the platform awaiting the train, and the day was cold. Every day in Wisconsin was cold, and I longed to go away, to go west. But Fader would not let me. Not until I was clean again.

Byron kept flicking looks at me. He began shuffling, slowly but determinedly, my way.

"Did your parents not want you either?" he asked me, when he had drawn close enough for talking.

I shook my head. I had not been in the country very long at that point and I was shy about the traces of my accent that still lingered, try as hard as I might to suppress them.

"You're nearly grown," he pointed out. "Why would they send you out for care now?"

"I don't need care. And it's rude to badger strangers."

Byron mulled on this for a moment. "I like your yellow hair." He reached up and grasped a small hank of his own hair. "It's like mine."

Our train that day did not come until long after dark. We were met at our destination by a very sour-faced girl a few years older than me. "I've half-froze out here waiting on you!" she snapped at the both of us. Byron tried to say something about the train, but I put my hand on his and he clammed right up.

Later I would teach him the first, most important rule of managing in a world that put you at a disadvantage: it was almost always better to listen than to speak.

The girl—Mrs. Rand's house girl—took us back to the farm that night. It was a big clapboard place with a porch skirting it all around. It was painted the color of lemon custard, and there were lacy white curtains in all of the windows. It was those pleasant white curtains that first made me suspicious. It seemed altogether too fine a place for me. I had never known Fader to lavish funds upon me, not when they could be spent on his own devouring needs.

"How much did your parents pay Mrs. Rand to take you on?"

"Less than she wanted for my little sister," Byron said. "That's why I was to go and not she."

"It's 'cause you're older," the house girl said carelessly. "She don't have to spend as much time caring for you, and she can send you out to work for other families or the like. And, pretty soon, she can send you out for good. You should see what she charges for a little baby. It would stop your heart."

* * *

We reconvened on the train to Arizona, all looking the worse for wear. Fader had not taken a drink in some fifteen hours by my count and he was in a very bad way, slumped in one corner of our berth with his eyes squeezed shut. One might have imagined he was asleep, but I could see the sickly sweat oozing from his skin. I could smell it, too, heady and fetid, like the fluid that issues from an infected wound.

Mamma was looking bloodless and big-eyed. To my eye, she looked something like a wild rabbit, poised to jump at the merest hint of danger. As for myself and Byron, we were both muddied from our less than proper disembarkation from the Texas train. I had snagged my dress on brambles in the darkness, and Byron was limping slightly, having landed badly on his right leg.

But we were still alive and free and we were headed for a new place—a clean place where we could start again.

"Mamma—" Byron started to say, and I nudged him.

"Remember," I said.

"Louisa," Byron corrected and Mamma frowned. "Did you bring me anything?"

I was surprised to see her reach into the velvet drawstring purse she carried on her wrist and produce a stubby little pencil.

She handed it over to him, saying "You can sharpen it with your knife."

Byron was pleased as he tucked the pencil into his coat. He was a great one for drawing pictures, especially of the animals. He would sit for hours if you let him, just sketching out pictures of the cows at their cuds.

"I do not care for the name Louisa," Mamma informed me icily.

"You can pick another."

"Another servant's name?"

Of course Mamma did not like our new plan. She disliked any plan that was not her own. Before we went out to the prairies, she had bridled at the thought of pretending to be a foreigner, no matter how often I told her it was for the benefit of us all. No one seriously questioned an old couple with only broken bits of English.

"It's not so very different from what we did in Michigan and Ohio, when I was the child medium of the Midwest."

"I was your mother in Michigan and Ohio," she hissed, "not your . . . handmaiden."

"You know we cannot travel as kin anymore. They're looking for a family, not for a celebrity spiritualist and her retinue. Besides, it won't be for very long."

Mamma sucked her lips into a pucker. What a proud creature she was! You would have thought she was born on a velvet pillow in a manor house, instead of coming up much like I had, doing the work she could get and never turning her nose up at a dollar. *Pretending* to be a lady's maid was far, far more dignified than some of things I knew her to have done for true.

"And we shall twiddle our thumbs, I suppose? While you charm that Nesbitt man and set yourself up nice and fine?"

She certainly knew—and I was not going to waste breath telling her—that ours was a business of give and take.

"You must trust me," I said instead. "And if you cannot, you know well enough now how to get off this train."

In all the time that I was there, I never heard anyone call it Whitewood Farm, which was just as well because I also never saw anyone farm anything there. Instead, everyone referred to it as the Lemon House, for its color. And everyone in town knew what the Lemon House was for.

The girls came in and the girls went out, almost constantly. They came with their big, protrudent bellies pointing the way forward, and they left deflated, half-hollowed out and sagging in all the places where their extra cargo had been.

I was determined that I wasn't going to get huge like them, and I certainly wasn't going to suffer like them. I heard their screams even when I was two floors above them, even when my door was tightly shut.

"Let down your burdens," Mrs. Rand said in the advertisements that she ran in the local and national papers, "in the house of a godly, discreet woman."

Mrs. Rand would take those burdens into her care

for a modest fee. Occasionally, she would take on older children like Byron, but when she did, she was sure to extract every penny from them by sending them out to the locals as farm and domestic labor. Everyone in the Lemon House knew their true value, every last cent of it.

Most of the babies were born dead, which made me hopeful. I had come there for the same reason that all those other women came: I was burdened. But I did not want to complete my pregnancy, not even in Mrs. Cecilia Rand's capable hands.

When I told her this, however, she made it very clear that I had no say in the matter. "Your father paid for your confinement and for the wee one. When you have the cash, I'll dance to your tune."

I didn't have any cash (I was young then and trusted Fader too much—I had not yet learned how to keep a little of our spoils back for myself), but I did have all the things I carried with myself: my keen eye, my sharp mind and my grinding, unceasing determination.

I knew Mrs. Rand did it—the thing I requested,

the thing I required above all others, because I had seen it happen. I had seen the girls come in with their glittery eyes flicking all around them, with their middles still waspish, their busy hands working nervously against one another. I had scrubbed their blood from the sheets and dumped their vomit out in the privy. I had watched them stagger home, often gray in the face and moving slowly but suffused with peace, with resolution. So I knew it was possible to vanish a pregnancy in the Lemon House. I simply had to find something that would move Mrs. Rand even more than the whisper of money.

I found it in the little blue baby.

The women who came to Mrs. Rand were not wealthy. Wealthy women could always find a place for their unexpected and unwanted offspring. For the rest of them, the poor and weak and luckless, there was the Lemon House.

The young ones would convince themselves that their son or daughter was even better off with Mrs. Rand and her lace curtains and her long front porch. The older women usually knew better but they had weighed the happiness of one child against the family entire and made the only decision they could.

Mrs. Rand claimed "affordable fees" in her advertisements, but many of the women were clearly offering her everything they had in the world. Some girls came to us so lean and hungry that we couldn't even tell they were with child until we stripped off their clothes.

The blue boy's mother, Klara, was like that. At first, I mistook her for one of the older women, so blasted and gray was her long face. Later, I found out she was only five years older than me. It had taken her so long, saving up for Mrs. Rand's fee, that she was nearly ready to burst by the time she made it to our door. She might even have been laboring as she stood, shaking in the winter cold but seemed to have no awareness of it. It was the first kind thing I ever saw Mrs. Rand do, when she picked up Klara in her thick arms like a little girl and carried her upstairs to the birthing room.

I never assisted with the births—that was the job of the house girl—but I did run back and forth, bringing up towels and dressings and water. They kept the room dark and humid with breath, and I kept getting little glimpses of the struggling woman on the bed and Mrs. Rand bent nervously over her nethers.

She never made a sound, that strange, lean woman. Not one scream.

"She's going to die," the house girl told me. Her arms were streaked with blood and there was some on her forehead and cheeks where she had hastily mopped at her sweat. "Her and the little one both, I'll wager."

But Klara did not die.

After nineteen hours in that dark room, she had delivered a dead baby, blue as the sky in summer with the cord around his neck like a noose. Before Mrs. Rand could bring the little creature down, however, there was a great commotion on the stairs. The starving woman was making her way down the stairs, mostly naked with a bundle of her clothing clutched to her nearly concave chest. Her stomach looked soft and awful, like the drooping paper wrappings on an ancient mummy and there was blood slicking her thighs, running in streams down to her feet. She left a trail of red as she staggered down the steps.

The housemaid tried to stop her. "You're not healed up yet, miss," the housemaid said, far gentler and more uncertain than I'd heard her say just about anything else.

Klara just kept moving toward the door as though she didn't even feel the maid's restraining hands on her. It seemed she had found a well of strength from somewhere other than—outside of—her own fragile body. The housemaid was a good sturdy girl, but this half-dead wisp of a woman dragged her helplessly across the foyer toward the front door.

When Klara got to the coat rack, she stopped for the first time, and her eyes seemed to sharpen, if only slightly. She stared at the coats hanging there, searching for her own, which was undoubtedly still up in the birthing room.

"Please," the housemaid said finally, "you're bleeding."

"It'll pass," she murmured, picking up one of the

coats. It belonged to one of the older boys, brown flannel and wool. She tugged it on over her nakedness, then she stepped into a pair of boots still wet with snow. They were Mrs. Rand's own pair and she would not be pleased about this, I thought.

"It was a sour belly," Klara said. "And now it's gone. Now there's nothing."

"But—" The housemaid grasped the back of Klara's stolen coat.

"Let her go." Mrs. Rand appeared on the stair's landing, her hands reddened in the same way the housemaid's had been.

The housemaid's face was crinkled with worry, but she released Klara's coat and allowed her to go to the door, to throw it open and step out into the still-falling snow. "She's going to bleed to death out there."

But I did not think she would. I did not think she would let herself.

Finally, the housemaid reached forward and shut the door, blocking out the frozen air. It was just then that there came from high above a perfect lusty cry, *piercing and loud and strong. Even Mrs. Rand started and we all looked toward the birthing room, where the dead baby was screaming for his mother.*

* * *

The baby still had the faintest bluish tinge when Mrs. Rand fetched him out of the birthing room, and he was small, to be sure. But his little hands were grasping in the air, and he was wailing high and bright.

Mrs. Rand recovered quickly, wrapping the tiny thing in a flannel and descending the stairs with him in her arms, much the way his mother had fled with her clothes tucked close to her. "I'll sit with him tonight. You rest your bones," she said to the bewildered housemaid.

The both of us craned our necks, almost involuntarily, to look upon the face of this dauntless little creature. He looked as most fresh-born children do: soft and compressed and filled with an inarticulate want.

Mrs. Rand did indeed sit with him that night in the

warm glow of the kitchen fire, feeding him warm goat's milk from a soaked rag instead of summoning one of the other girls still nursing. The next morning when we came down for breakfast, we found her sitting at the table still, but now with a mug of black coffee at her elbow and no child in sight.

"He didn't make it," she said, her eyes raccooned with sleeplessness.

The housemaid tsked and went to fetch her apron. "I knew it," she said. "That little thing was born weak."

I did not say anything but only drifted over to the wash bucket, where Mrs. Rand had disposed of the rag. Without even lifting it to my nose, I could smell melting sugar burn of brandy and beneath that something bitter and unmistakable. Laudanum.

· · ·

"How many of them were really stillborn?" I asked Mrs. Cynthia Rand once, some time later. She didn't

hesitate for a moment before telling me. "That is not important. Those children were bitterly unwanted. Those 'mothers' were never going to think of their off-spring but to shudder with shame and horror. Every woman who walks into this house has one great wish: for their child to disappear. To cease to be. All I did was grant their wish."

I thought of some of the girls I had seen in the Lemon House even in just the short time I had been there. There was the girl who worked in the saloon in the town who brought us a three- year-old girl with a brand new ribbon woven into her plait. She came to visit every weekend until the poor little thing died. "Pneumonia," Mrs. Rand had said. It was something terrible and wasting at least.

And then there was the young woman who had no English but huge, expressive green eyes. She had wailed and sobbed while an older woman dragged her out of the house, infant daughter in the housemaid's arms.

Even Byron claimed his parents had been "real good" to him. They had promised him that Mrs. Rand was a kind woman, a godly woman, and she would give him a sure and comfortable home. They did not know that he spent his days doing the work of a full-grown man for every farm family in the county.

"Do you think a woman like that," Mrs. Rand had said when I confronted her with my suspicions about the blue boy's death, "would keep paying room and board for that child? She didn't even have the upfront fee, barely half of it."

It was very easy to understand Mrs. Rand once I knew one simple truth about her: she cared more for a dollar than for any living being. Whenever someone walked through her door, she made a quick and shrewd calculation. Were they likely to pay? Were they likely to keep paying? Were they going to check in on their little ones? Were they going to kick up a fuss if something went sideways, and would they be believed if they did?

I appealed to this math when I went about securing my own desires. I was still alive and well in the Lemon House, so Fader must have been making his *payments regularly. However, he had neither sent word nor appeared in person since sending me away from the city. I knew why, though Mrs. Rand could not. I still remembered how he had looked at me before I left, how he had told me so sadly, "I hate the sight of you."*

I knew he would not come to visit, certainly not to see the child. But he would pay. "He will pay," I said, "whether the creature is born or not."

I did not say—did not need to say—that were she to deny me, I would expose her to the community for an infanticide.

Together, we took nearly $200 from Fader, split less than evenly between the two of us. Almost a year later, when I confronted him with that money, money Mrs. Rand and I had used to fly far from the Lemon House and set up as a youthful medium and her doting mother, he had laughed and laughed at me.

He was still laughing when I wiped the vomit from his chin and helped him back to the fine hotel where Mrs. Rand and I were staying. It felt good to see his disintegration, how far he had fallen in my absence, and how fast. I think we both knew then that he would not be sending me away ever, ever again.

Mrs. Rand, who insisted I call her "Mother," said we didn't need him.

"I know," I said. "He needs us."

•   •   •

Nesbitt's Creek had until very recently been called Dead Horse Creek because, like many places, the most important thing that had ever happened there was also the worst thing that ever happened there. It was a nowhere outpost in New Mexico territory with some minor copper seams and a bitter, poisoned lake to draw in unwary travelers.

That was until Royal Nesbitt, a wealthy speculator from the Midwest had come out and discovered an incredible deposit of silver, enough to make him a millionaire many times over. He promptly renamed the settlement Nesbitt's Creek and began building it into a town proper with hotels and gaming halls and fine houses and ranches.

I first encountered him in a newspaper that Mamma brought back from Ellston, where she regularly went to sell some of our takings from the inn. *SILVER BARON SEEKS ADVICE FROM THE OTHER SIDE*, it said, and the story went on to describe Nesbitt's staunch belief in the spirit realm. It was a medium's advice, he claimed, that had led him to the incredible silver bonanza that had made his fortune.

I squirreled that newspaper away, though Mamma was the only one who might have been able to read it. Nesbitt's Creek was going to be mine, like the bag around my waist. It was so perfectly suited to my talents that it almost suggested the influence of a higher power.

But then came the doctor from back east, and I had to abandon those ambitions for the good of the family. Without me, who would guide Byron and make sure he spent his time industriously, rather than on frivolous pursuits? Who would check Mamma's temper and keep her from raging at the neighbors and guests? Who would calibrate Fader's liquor precisely enough to keep him cogent but cheerful? Without me, every one of them would surely have perished.

I had never seen the desert before, so I willed myself to stay awake while the others dozed in their seats. I pressed my face tight against the cold glass of the train window and tried to make out the contours of the new land where we would make our home.

The desert was blue-black and endless, all twisting stone and the unimaginably distant promise of scrubby trees. It seemed to belong to a different nation from the prairie grasslands and it felt as though we were leaving that whole life behind us, a hollowed out skin of the sort a snake leaves in its wake. I looked at them, my sleeping family, and I was proud knowing that I had saved them; I protected them and kept them. Me and no one else.

6

Unpleasant Things

Lawce Gibbon
Madalane, Kansas
February, 1872

We knew that the Drakes were different. We believed they were thieves. We had even suspected that they had murdered that poor doctor from the east. But we never imagined they were monsters.

A group of men, including Charlie and Pap, camped out at the Drake's homestead, sleeping in their rigs because no one could tolerate a night in that charnel house. The rest of us went back to Madalane to round up all the able-bodied men we could find.

All the lights in the store were blazing when we

walked inside. I was confronted by a wall of warm air from the hard-working woodstove. It was Ma, I'm sure, who had set everything up and kept the women—and it was nearly all women sitting or standing anxiously inside the store—comfortable.

Ma set a kettle back on the stove where it belched steam in protest. She came over to me just as a number of the other women arose as well, either to approach their men or ask word of them. Katie Conkle was there as well. She did not rush over but her eyes were on me alone.

"Son," was all my mother said, touching my face like an apology.

Next to the stove, the widow had not moved. I gave Ma's arm a squeeze and moved past her to kneel at the widow's feet. In front of me, I could see nothing but the silken black expanse of her mourning dress.

"I'm so sorry," I said.

When I finally gathered my courage to look up at her, I found her eyes glittering oddly, as though they were made of a thousand sharp planes designed to catch the light. "The little girl as well? My child," her voice broke, "too?"

"It is likely."

The sound she made was not a sob or a cry but altogether lower and more damaged. It sounded like the noise an animal would make upon discovering its limb was hopelessly pinned in a cruel human trap.

She swayed in her seat like a drunkard, and I was so glad that Ma was there to catch her up because I felt a sudden but intense aversion to touching the widow woman. It was almost as if her misery would infect me or co-mingle with my own horror and combust in some terrible fashion.

"What are we to do now?" Katie spoke for the first time, still unmoving from her place next to the penny candy barrels.

"I've come to fetch whichever men feel they can come along," I told her and the rest of them. "We have work to do out at the Drake place."

. . .

By the time we had raised a dozen more men from their beds and convinced them to head out into the cold, it was coming on daylight. Kate insisted on going, though we all tried to dissuade her.

"It's awful, Katie," I said. "There's nothing good in it, nothing moral or redeeming. Going out there will not benefit you in even the smallest way."

She looked at me hard. "You need hands and mine are as good as anyone else's."

When we got to the homestead, most everyone was out in the orchard. The men had shovels and picks to work at the mounds and uncover whatever evil thing was concealed underneath. A few others— Katie amongst them—examined the house and the outbuildings again, combing through everything for a hint to where the Drakes might have gone.

A very small group, headed by the sheriff himself, went off on an errand unknown. When I asked Pap what they were doing, he just shook his head and directed me back toward the heap of hard brown dirt between us.

The ground was near froze and none too eager to give up its secrets. It took two men just to excavate a single mound. Fortunately—for us at least—it seemed that the Drakes had encountered the very same problem and had only concealed their awful business between a few feet of earth.

The grave Pap and I were working on was the newest with no plant growth atop it, the doctor's likely resting place. Pap swung his pick at the mound as though it were stone rather than dirt, and I scooped up the loosened dirt and moved it to one side. We exposed what appeared to be a pair of pale, naked legs; feet without the dignity of shoes or socks.

The cold air had kept him from putrefying, but as more and more of him appeared from under the frosty dirt, I wondered if that was any better. It was eerie to look at him lying there, like a pale sleeper in a bed of dust.

We freed his face first, which was a mistake. From then on, his staring, clouded eyes watched us attentively as we worked. I tried to look only at the end of my own shovel, but I could still feel his dead stare.

When we got to his chest, there was some difficulty. Or rather, a lack of difficulty. The dirt cover there was so shallow, little more than a light dusting over a small but protruding shape. Pap abandoned his pick and knelt down to brush the dirt away with his bare hands.

Unlike the man, the little girl was nearly fully dressed, missing only the hat that any loving mother would have tied upon her before letting her out in winter. She was pressed to her father's stripped chest in a way that seemed both obscene and ancient, like one of those writhing marble statues of the old, dead gods I had seen in my schoolbooks.

One of her hands was stretched upwards toward her father's face. Her fingers were locked into a fist with some of his hair and a good portion of dirt inside it. Her face was the same gray-blue as the man's but where his expression was blank nothingness, she had a look of bewildered frustration about her.

Her mouth was open and there was dirt inside, as well as smeared around her lips. They had tossed her into her father's grave alive, leaving her to choke on mud in the freezing cold.

Pap opened his own mouth, though I could not imagine what he could possibly say in the face of this discovery. Instead, we were interrupted by the urgent sound of hoof beats as Harris came tearing onto the property. His hat was gone, presumably blown off in his haste, and his unbuttoned coat was fluttering in the bitter air. As he drew closer, I noticed a length of rope tied off to the back of his saddle. At the end of the rope was an indistinguishable dark shape, moving—writhing—under its own power.

"We got 'em!" Harris pulled the horse up short in the middle of the orchard. The sheriff appeared around the side of the Drakes' house on his own nag, moving at a noticeably slower clip. The thing on the end of Harris's rope was still moving and reconfiguring itself until I could make out a face, bleeding and dirty but recognizably human.

"Goddammit," the sheriff glowered at Harris, who had hopped down from his mount and was working at the knot on the back of his saddle. "You could have killed him, Parsons, and then what use would he be?"

Harris laughed. "He's hardy, I can tell." Knot undone, he grabbed the freed end of the rope and used it to pull the person—a young man—up onto his feet. Harris had looped the rope around his waist as well as tied his clasped hands together. Though the man's face was wet with blood and bruises were raising up on his chin and throat, he was able to move and walk without visible pain.

"Tom Larsson?" Abner said, dropping his shovel by one of the other graves and moving toward Harris's horse. I recognized the name; the Larssons were a large family of Swedes with a complement of young folks too numerous to name. They kept a small farm on the Little Blossom Creek to the west; if the Drakes could be said to have neighbors, the Larsson family was it.

"He's that Drake bitch's sweetheart," Harris sneered, pulling Tom Larsson forward roughly. The boy began to mumble something, a soft demurral.

"I know that boy," Abner Conkle said sternly. "He does all the business for the family, comes into the hotel on occasion. He's a real polite boy."

"We heard he was infatuated with the Drake daughter," the sheriff said.

"He followed her around like a goddamned dog!" Harris insisted.

Abner shook his head. "That is true enough, I suppose."

"You think he knows where they went?" Pap asked, stepping out of the doctor's grave and approaching the horses.

The sheriff opened his mouth but Harris beat

him to it. "I'm sure of it. Would you let your woman go off without telling you where she was headed? Besides, he's going to stick by his people, ain't he?"

"They aren't," Tom said, his voice a wounded rasp. It was the first time he'd spoken intelligibly since the horses approached. He had a very mild accent. "The Drakes aren't Swedes, not all of them. Just the old man. And Em." He winced as he said her name, as though anticipating a blow.

"How do you figure?" the sheriff asked, his voice admirably gentle.

"They couldn't speak to us and couldn't understand us when we spoke. The old woman would pretend. The boy didn't even try."

The sheriff screwed up his face until wrinkles sprouted on his forehead. "Why would they lie about something like that?"

"Didn't want to talk to folks, I suppose. I never asked."

"Never asked about much, did ya?" Harris snorted.

"Did you know what they were doing here?" Pap demanded, pushing past Harris to get right close to the boy.

"Lawrence—" the sheriff began.

"No, Sheriff, you go over there where Lawce is standing, and you look at what they did here. If he had any part of it, so help me . . . "

The sheriff approached the partially uncovered grave with a blank face, as though he already knew exactly what he was going to see there. When he looked down at the little girl, coiled against her daddy, he drew in a single tight breath.

Curious, Charlie ambled over from the grave he had been uncovering with Abner. Soon, they were all crowding the little shallow hole where I still stood in six inches of loose dirt. A strange noise came up from the gathered men as they looked at the grave, a gut-punched moan.

"Did you know?" Pap was asking the boy again, taking hold of the rope still tied around him and drawing Tom close to his own face.

"I . . . I knew they robbed," Tom stammered. "They had too much. Fine things and no reason for how they got them. I figured they took from the ones who stayed overnight."

Charlie looked up from the grave; his cheeks were bright red, though I could not tell if that was from the winter cold or from the blood rising in his face. He stomped away from the gravesite toward our father and the tied boy.

Without saying a word, Charlie grabbed a portion of the slack rope and looped it easily around the boy's neck, like he was an old friend throwing an arm around his shoulder. The boy reacted too late, and Charlie had pulled his improvised noose tight before Tom could even get a finger between the rope and his neck. "You knew they were thieves and said naught to anyone?" Charlie demanded, half-shouting so everyone could hear.

Tom said nothing—likely he could not say anything—and just scrabbled at the rope with his fingernails. "How did you think they were taking those things, eh? Did you suppose folks just let them steal all their earthly belongings?"

"More concerned with getting under Em Drake's skirts than helping his fellow man," Harris agreed. Tom had stopped moving now, frozen, and was watching Harris's face with wide eyes.

"Tell us where they went and we will have no quarrel with you," Harris said, almost smiling. It seemed so strange to me that this was the same boy I had shared a schoolroom with for so many years.

Harris looked at Charlie, who immediately slackened the rope around Tom's neck, as though the two had rehearsed this action earlier. "I don't know," Tom pleaded, "I never knew. She never told me nothing. She cared not a bit for me, though I loved her—"

Charlie pulled the rope viciously, knocking Tom to his knees. This only put more pressure on the rope, and while the boy dug at his neck desperately, his movements were languid and weak. Charlie let him hang there, and we could all see the bluish pallor come over his face.

I looked at the sheriff, who was still standing next to me and the other men by the grave. "You aren't going to do anything about this?" I muttered.

"Sometimes unpleasant things need doing." The sheriff frowned.

I looked around the informal circle of men and saw similar conclusions in their faces. Before us, Tom writhed and his nostrils quivered, desperately trying to suck life from the air.

"Enough," Harris said and Charlie slacked the rope again. Tom collapsed fully onto his hands and knees and retched awfully. A little puddle of something that might have once been cornmeal mash appeared on the ground between his palms.

Pap reared back suddenly and gave the boy a kick, square in the stomach. He vomited again and this time it was streaked with blood. "The Drakes are gonna die for what they've done," Pap advised the young man. "And we have no compunction about doing the same for those that helped them. You don't want to be someone who helped them, do you, son?"

"Blossom Valley?" Tom sobbed into the dirt. "The train station?"

"That a question or an answer?" Charlie demanded but all he got from Tom was another pitiful sob. Charlie pulled the rope again and Tom's chin tilted back until we were all looking at his wild eyes and his mouth smeared with vomit.

We are watching him die, I realized.

Before I could do anything (or perhaps I was merely comforting myself, imagining that I was going to do something) Katie emerged from the Drakes' homestead and made an awful, piercing scream.

Everything stopped. Charlie dropped the rope, and Tom hit the dirt and curled in on himself. All heads save Tom's turned toward Katie, who was as pale as candle wax and had tears in her eyes. "What in the holy hell are you doing?" she demanded. I saw

Abner Conkle look down at his feet, ashamed of his loud and vulgar daughter.

"Katie, this is no business of yours," Charlie started.

"This is my business, Charlie Blake, and the business of every person in Madalane. Don't we have a courthouse? Don't we have a judge?" She directed this last question at the sheriff, who suddenly found something important to examine in the dirt near the doctor's feet.

"No time for all that." Harris's voice was surprisingly gentle. "We need to know where the Drakes are headed."

"Nesbitt's Creek," Katie said promptly, producing a folded bit of newsprint, soft and delicate with age. I approached to get a better look at it, and she pointed at the headline. "See? Rich fella leans on false mediums like they speak the gospel truth. That'd be like catnip for Emmelene Drake."

"Where did you find this?"

"It was tucked up with her stockings and

underthings." Well, that was certainly a place that we would not have searched on our own.

"Why were you looking in there?" Charlie took the newspaper out of her hands and showed it to Harris and Pap, who regarded it warily.

Katie looked at Charlie like he was the dumbest creature on God's good Earth, and I had never wanted to kiss her more than in that moment. "Did you ever have dealings with the old couple or the boy?"

Charlie shook his head.

"That's because Emmelene was the one that made the decisions. *Emmelene* was the smart one, and so Emmelene would be the one with a plan."

"We have to warn these people," I told Pap, gesturing at the newspaper. The people of Nesbitt's Creek were sitting unawares and unprepared for the storm that was about to come upon them. After being exposed here in Madalane, the Drakes were, if anything, even more desperate. And more dangerous.

Pap shook his head. "No. If we send word it might get back to the Drakes. They have a day or more on us already. If they get spooked and leave Nesbitt's Creek, we'll never find them."

"But what if they hurt folks there? Kill them?" I thought of the girl in the grave, such a little thing. She had no treasures or money. She could not have told their secrets or witnessed against them. She was killed simply because her presence was inconvenient. She died an awful death—choking in a dark hole— just to make their lives a tiny bit easier.

"We'll have to get there fast," Pap said grimly. "Before they get the chance."

7

Signs and Manifestations

Emmelene Drake
Nesbitt's Creek, New Mexico Territory
February, 1872

Gossip could outstrip even a train, apparently, and we arrived in Nesbitt's Creek some days after rumors of our doings in Kansas. Of course, those doings did not exactly belong to us anymore. They were the work of the Drake family, who were strangers to us, Miss Zenia Olginskaya and her faithful maid Louisa.

I sent Byron into town as a young speculator shopping for claims with his enfeebled grandfather. Fader more than looked the part. They were to book a modest room on the second floor in the hotel while Mamma and I would rent the large downstairs suite.

The town was still much more of a Dead Horse Creek than a Nesbitt's Creek, and it was far smaller than Madalane had been. But the hotel was new and well appointed and not very far from Nesbitt's mansion, a great beast of a house still under construction.

The people in the streets were a queer mixture of rough adventuring sorts and moneyed people—or people looking to get moneyed—who had been attracted by the new buildings and the rail line.

I kept having to remind Mamma to walk behind me instead of automatically striding out in front as was her habit. Though it ran contrary to everything we had spent the last few days doing, I wanted very much to be seen as we made our way from the train station to the hotel.

I had put what Mamma and the others believed to be the lion's share of our assets into a very specific wardrobe for myself—for Zenia—and though it must have galled Mamma to no end, she had said nothing against it. For our procession to the hotel,

I wore an enormous silk hat with glistening white orchids pinned to it.

I looked straight ahead as we made our way toward the hotel, but out of the corners of my eyes, I could see people pausing to watch as we passed. I did not smile, though, for Zenia was always fierce or distant, listening to the spectral voices.

In the hotel, we got our first indication of how famous we had become. The newspapers there had large front-page stories about our exploits, and some even promised *IMAGES FROM THE HAUNTING SCENE!*

Mamma's face went white when she noticed the paper in a small wooden rack. Fortunately, a certain blanching was not unreasonable for one confronted with such unpleasantness so early in the day.

The hotel's desk attendant was a slim, excitable young man whose eyes gleamed when we swept through the door. "Ladies," he said, "welcome to the Silkwater Hotel. How can I help you today?"

I gave him a queenly nod while Mamma tried

not to stare at the newspaper. I touched her forearm and she turned to the attendant to say, "My mistress requires a suite, the largest you have, please. Suitable for hosting salons."

The attendant's eyes dilated either with excitement or avarice. "Salons? How interesting. I assume you all are Easterners?"

Mamma nodded.

"Are you folks . . . " He paused and looked at me, taking in everything from the tips of my white fox fur to the inch of brown leather boot visible underneath my skirt. " . . . performers?"

Mamma painted a scandalized look across her face. "I should say not! The service my mistress provides is very serious and very real. It is not . . . entertaining." She spat the last word like a foul, dripping thing.

"What does she do?" the attendant half whispered, as though I were not present or were in some way insensible.

"She pierces the veil," Mamma said earnestly.

Seeing the attendant's bewildered look, she added, "She sees through to the other side and returns messages from the dead."

"Goodness!" the attendant gave a merry little hand clap. "You are in the right place, ladies. You know the Indians in these parts say that this place is a sacred place, a ghostly place. I suppose that is why you have come?"

I gave him a slow-blossoming and mysterious smile, which I had perfected in hundreds of mirrors from Michigan to New Mexico territory, and said in Zenia's thick accent, "I came because I was called."

• • •

Each newspaper offered slightly different information about the villainous Drake family and their dark deeds. Some called us bandits; others termed us a family of "the most depraved lunatics." One claimed that the bodies had been "tortured and mutilated," while others wrote of the dead men's hauntingly perfect countenances. They gave estimates of anywhere between eight and twenty dead at the homestead.

My own recollection was that the true number was somewhere in between.

In our suite—which was more than serviceable and offered a very comprehensive view of the town's main artery—we hoarded all the newspapers we could find. I sent Byron out to collect them from businesses on the street, and I read aloud excerpts from the stories about us when he would no longer accept my assurances that the papers were of little consequences. I spared him the frequent descriptions of him as the "idiot son" of the "demented band of killers."

"That's not right," he said, after a particularly harrowing description of the state of some of the bodies. "We took no joy in it. That's not true. How can they print things like that? Lies?"

"It is something that happened to someone else," I said as gently as I could. "In another life.

Lars"—for that is the new name I had given him—"has no care for the reputation of the Drake family."

The second, far more important task I had given Byron was to find out all that he could about Royal Nesbitt and his movements. As one might imagine from a town that bore his name, Nesbitt's Creek was very attentive to Mr. Nesbitt himself.

He was not at present in the town or the territory, as he had apparently been managing his business interests abroad for the past several months. "Folks think he's coming back soon, though," Byron told me. "They say he always spends the spring here."

Best of all, when he did arrive, he was almost certain to take supper at the hotel's restaurant. "He always eats his first supper here," Byron added. "He's religious about it."

"No, he's superstitious about it. But that's even better."

Royal Nesbitt's imminent arrival was all but a certainty, and we had only to place ourselves in the dining room at the correct time. Until then, we could focus on developing Zenia's reputation as a psychic without peer.

To that end, I had Mamma place paper advertisements in the lobby of the hotel. *SIGNS and MANIFESTATIONS! Guaranteed GUIDANCE from the realm of the ETERNAL!* And below: *Madame Professor Zenia Olginskaya answers ALL questions, call at Suite 106.* I did not think it would be long before we had our first clients. A mining town is a believing town. Who else would abandon their lives and travel all these perilous miles for a chance to sift dirt in the bottom of a hole? Only the faithful, the deluded, and the truly rock stupid: the same folks who had always filled out my séance table.

•   •   •

Over the next few days, I blessed countless stones, spoons, cups, hats, and even a false tooth, so that they might offer the bearer luck in their endeavors. I comforted a plump widow with news that her young husband was "much at peace" in the land beyond. He was there with his own father and their little babe. I told the front desk attendant that a woman named Eliza or Elizabeth was forever at his shoulder, watching over him. "Granny?" he had enthused, nearly in tears.

My most impressive achievement, however, was clearly my "healing" of George Keystone's (née Fader) ulcerous leg. I performed this wonder in the parlor of the hotel where a sizable crowd gathered to watch me work.

I gave them a good show for their efforts, sweating and toiling over Fader's bare leg for nearly a quarter of an hour. I drew forth individuals from the crowd until we encircled Fader, and I asked them to open themselves to the spirit world, to allow themselves to become mere conduits of energy.

After that, it was a very simple matter to use a discreet handkerchief and the laying on of hands to wipe the congealed pork fat, flour paste, and animal blood Mamma had used to fashion his "weeping wound" from Fader's skin.

Afterwards, folks surged toward me, each one of them bearing some incredible misery that they hoped I could alleviate. Mamma guided me out of the room while I pretended to swoon against her. My ministrations required considerable effort, and it would be some time before I could duplicate my work on Fader's leg.

The crowd's reaction to my performance with Fader assured me that no one else in Nesbitt's Creek was offering anything of the same caliber. My confidence was further rewarded the very next day when a note was delivered to suite requesting Zenia's presence at a formal dinner that evening with Mr. Royal Nesbitt and his companion.

"And how much will that cost?" Mamma sniffed when I showed her the note. I was surprised at how stubborn and sour Mamma could be. I had believed that even she would not be able to deny that this was a small triumph, a signal that our plan was working smoothly and effectively.

"I presume Mr. Nesbitt will pay, but the supper

prices are listed in the lobby. You may consult them at your leisure."

Mamma went over to the large steamer trunk we had purchased to store Zenia's wardrobe and began wrathfully picking through the frocks hanging there. "And which of these shall you wear? Do you need jewelry? Perhaps a diamond necklace? Or a tiara, maybe?"

"This is not a social endeavor. I am working for you and for Fader and for Byron."

Mamma nodded, her face very placid and reasonable, which was how I knew she was about to be particularly disagreeable. "Certainly. And while you are *working* so selflessly for us, we sit here unprotected, bleeding money."

I forced a laugh, and it was hollow and too high, the sound a witch might make. "And what would you do instead? Divvy up the take and go our own ways? Father to the bottle and Byron to the devil. And you—would you wind up in the asylum again, eh?"

I spoke softly, almost kindly, but she nevertheless looked as though I had slapped her with my open hand. She always said she had done it a-purpose, to be spared the noose when some folk in another state discovered the smaller, less organized baby farm she had operated in her youth. She claimed to know ways of madness and to be able to ape its symptoms. "A great trick," she called it, but one she had always shied away from subsequently. I had always wondered just how feigned her madness really was.

"Go to your dinner," she spit, making for the suite's front door. "You need not concern yourself with my welfare."

And so I did not.

•　•　•

I had been imagining Royal Nesbitt as a young man, perhaps not much older than I. And he certainly wasn't aged, but he did have a strange and disconcerting mixture of young and old about him at the same time. He had an infant's round, unformed face and widely spaced teeth, but his head was nearly bald with just a few spindly wisps of hair stretched across his pale scalp and twin tufts over his ears. He had bright, alert blue eyes along with the reddened eyelids of a long-time drinker. When he saw me enter the parlor he smiled, and his lips were very red and curiously shiny, as though he licked them incessantly.

He stood up from his table and threw his arms out to either side as though to greet me in a great clasping. Zenia was not partial to physical contact with strangers and neither was Emmelene, so I merely nodded to him and gave him a small smile of my own. "Madame Professor!" he said, his voice surprisingly high.

"Mr. Nesbitt."

He pulled a chair away from the table, and I occupied it graciously. It was then that I noticed the other woman for the first time. She was staring into her water glass like into a looking glass. Unlike

Nesbitt, it was immediately clear that she was well and truly a young person, with a fresh, scrubbed face and a slender build. She wore a dress the color of rust, and her dark hair was pillowed elegantly around her long, albeit striking face. Her skin was dark, and being this close to the border, I supposed she was from Mexican stock.

She seemed to sense my stare and looked up at me briefly, almost apologetically, before turning her attention to the silverware.

"Of course," Royal Nesbitt said, settling in between the two of us, "how could I be so rude? Madame Professor, this is . . . " He paused and offered to the girl the silly gaze of a desperately love-sick man. " . . . my most important and beloved bit of charity." He seemed very pleased with this summation.

"My ward!" he added with a laugh. "Lucille Bonheur."

"Good evening, Madame," Lucille said. Her

voice was as low and liquid as her companion's was oddly piercing.

"A pleasure, Mademoiselle."

"Yes, I've been looking after Lucy since she was just a wee mite," Nesbitt said fondly. Lucille did not look up from the silverware and the silence bristled with discomfort, but Nesbitt himself did not seem to notice. He kept staring at Lucille until he got his fill. Then he turned abruptly to me and stuck his pointer finger in my face.

"You!" he said. His fingers were very round—his hands in general were plump—but they came to a pronounced point at the ends, something like a carrot. "You have been making quite the spectacle in my little town, eh?

"I give assistance. To those who ask for it."

The hotel attendant, who also apparently managed the restaurant, appeared at my elbow. As ever, he radiated a barely contained thrill at the very presence of his social superiors. "Madame." He gave me an absurd little bow. "Mr. Nesbitt," he added with considerably more warmth, and then he turned to look at Lucille, who seemed to have him at a loss. "Miss," he settled on finally, giving her a nod, "this is Lucille!"

Nesbitt boomed. "And she shall soon enough be the mistress of this town, so you must learn her face."

The attendant nodded vigorously, a man absorbing a number of very wise admonitions. He turned his attention toward Lucille, much to her visible chagrin. "I'll not forget you, Miss," he said earnestly.

"Gin," I interrupted, hoping to banish the little creature. "Please."

Nesbitt grinned at me. "I'll have the same," he said, while Lucille demurred. "My apologies for the service," Nesbitt added. "We are still a rough place in many ways."

I waved this away graciously.

"In fact . . . " Nesbitt made a great show of rubbing his chin and left jowl in deep thought. "I do wonder what has drawn you to Nesbitt's Creek? We must seem very meager and gauche to someone like yourself, who has undoubtedly traveled the world."

When I looked at him, I made sure that my eyes were as large and earnest as I could muster. "Mr. Nesbitt, I came to this place for you."

He tried, but he could not hide the little shock of delight that moved through him at my words. Royal Nesbitt was clearly the sort of man who believed that the universe had set out a special destiny just for him.

"Multiple spirits came to me and proffered your name," I continued in my most mystical tone. "They said you were beginning a great enterprise and that they had vital information for you."

Nesbitt was leaning toward me now, unintentionally, I was sure. Beside him, Lucille was paying closer attention to me, but unlike Nesbitt, she showed nothing of her feelings in her face.

"What sort of information?" Nesbitt demanded.

I lowered my head and shook it sadly. "They will

not say. They must tell you directly. And that, sir, is why I had to come to Nesbitt's Creek."

The momentary silence stretched out, hanging heavy over the table until Nesbitt leaned back away from me and cracked a wide smile packed with his odd baby teeth. "This is wonderful!" he said in the same booming voice he had used to introduce Lucille. "We shall have a proper séance now, darling." He reached out and grasped Lucille's hand, giving it a warm pump with his own fingers. "With both you and Madame Olginskaya at the table, I can only imagine the kind of channels we may open into the other world." My eyebrows shot up. "Your lady is a medium as well?" I had not counted on Nesbitt having a companion, let alone one who fancied herself a table-rapper, and it was the sort of complication that I could do without.

"Oh, not a medium, exactly. But sensitive. Very sensitive." Nesbitt lowered his voice, the next sentence a delectable secret between us three. "She has that wild blood, you know. Indians are a very spiritual people."

So not a Mexican maiden, then. That explained her Easterner accent. "You're an Indian?" I asked mildly. Lucille opened her mouth to answer but, as I imagined he often did, Nesbitt beat her to it.

"Her father was an Ojibwa chief and her mother was a beautiful Frenchwoman. Some said she had a bit of blue blood from way back. The chief fell in love with her from afar and snatched her away from a settlement and made her his squaw." His eyes gleamed.

For the first time, Lucille's face evinced a clear emotion. I could see the dark crimson blush overtaking her cheeks, though whether it was rage, embarrassment or some heady combination, I could not tell.

"Somehow, the folks at the Indian school got ahold of her and tried to raise her up, but they couldn't see what they had in her." Whenever he looked at her, a kind of helplessness seemed to overtake him, like a little boy gazing upon his mother with naked, unblemished admiration. "They were trying to teach her to be a maid or a seamstress," he laughed. "Can you imagine? Could they not see her aristocratic mien?"

He was still holding Lucille's right hand but her left was clenched in an ugly fist, her thumbnail working at the soft skin around her fingers. She dug deep around her middle finger, and a perfect pearl of blood appeared on her brown skin. I watched it grow and grow until it became a trickle and then a drip and then a stain on the white tablecloth.

She jerked her hand suddenly at the appearance of the drip and jostled her water glass, sending it spilling across the table. Lucille jumped up, and Nesbitt began to laugh, a laugh that he seemed to draw upwards from the very depths of his belly.

"My shy girl!" he said, taking both sides of her face in his hands. "What a delicate thing!"

●　●　●

I expected silence and darkness when I returned

to the suite that night. Mamma, having had her tantrum, was sure to be either sleeping off drink or wrathfully pretending to do the same. Instead, I opened the door to the suite to find a blaze of lamps and Mamma sitting upright and straight-backed at the small writing desk provided to us. She was turned toward the door, and I wondered how long she had waited there, expecting me.

She said nothing to me. In fact, she barely moved. She simply lifted her arm and allowed to dangle in the air the little cache-purse where I had so long been hoarding my special share of our monies. I wore it always around my waist, but Zenia did not because it surely would have ruined the silhouette of all her fine gowns.

Mamma let the bag swing slightly, like a dead man in a tree, and began to smile. I stepped into the room and shut the door behind me.

8

Survivors

Lawce Gibbon and Emmelene Drake
Nesbitt's Creek, New Mexico Territory
February, 1872

"**Y**ou ever been on a train before?" Somehow, Harris and I had wound up in the same section of the squat little passenger car. He perched on the relative opulence of the train seat like a man waiting for a gunshot.

"A few times," I admitted. "Trips with Pap." Those trips were mostly to negotiate with suppliers and potential business contacts.

"Never have." He leaned over me uncomfortably to watch the land outside slide by. "Not sure how I like it."

Out the window, the sun had turned into a

scorching pink ball, perfectly outlined against the blue of the sky.

"No one forced you on the train." Harris had been one of the first to step forward when Pap and the sheriff asked for a few men to come to Nesbitt's Creek and intercept the Drakes before they could do even more damage.

"Nah," he murmured, still leaning over me. "Gotta see this through."

"Why?" The question came out of my mouth unbidden. It was a query, though, that I had been nurturing since I had first seen Harris take charge of the hunting party so hot upon the heels of his own humiliation at the hand of mostly the same men.

Harris settled back in his proper seat.

"Did you know Lena's husband, Henry?" he asked.

"Only to say hello," I said. "He seemed like a good enough man."

Harris's face darkened. "He wasn't. Did you

know he used to beat her bloody? Curse her and spit on her when she was down?"

I had not known that. There were men in town who were well known to have a heavy hand with their women, but I had never heard that of Henry Klein. And Lena hardly seemed the sort of woman to be so profaned. Women who got cuffed or whipped by their men tended toward the slatternly and the wicked. Lena was by all accounts a good woman who would give no good man reason to strike her.

"He wasn't ever going to stop, not until she was dead. Or he was." Harris fell silent, looking at me as though begging me not to make him speak plain.

"So," I said finally, "you chose?"

Harris nodded and made a sound in his throat like a sob cut short before it could really begin.

"I heard it was an accident, when Henry . . . " I could not complete the thought. To do so would somehow conjure the idea into being, make it a part of the real world that must then be addressed properly.

"I chose. For her." Harris's voice was small but unwavering. It was not an apology.

"And the men that came for you?"

Harris nodded. "They had cause, yes. Though I am glad they didn't string me up in the end." That was as close to a "thank you" as I would ever get from him, I imagined.

"Lena had nothing to do with it," he added, suddenly and with considerably more fire. "I don't even think she knows what really happened. Though sometimes I wonder . . . "

"She is a good woman," he added softly. "She deserved better."

"But all this," I waved my hand toward the sinking sun out the window and the prim little train car itself, "has nothing to do with you or Lena, surely?"

Harris surprised me by letting out a big, hale laugh of the sort I might have heard from him when we were both youngsters. "You think that when we ride back into Madalane with those butchers in tow anyone is going to talk—or think—of anything else for the rest of our lives?"

I awoke to a hard poke in my side and the crinkle of newspaper.

"I know this word," Byron said, leaning over me like a hag come to steal my breath in a dream. He jabbed his finger at another headline about the Drake family, at the word *CANNIBALS*.

I sighed and pressed my face into my pillow. Undeterred, Byron climbed into the bed next to me. It had been more than two weeks since we had all dozed together like this; he must have been missing it. He curled his body against mine.

"I had the man at the front desk read it to me," he whispered.

"You know you shouldn't do that," I admonished him, my voice muffled from the pillow.

He wriggled in closer to me, encircling my waist

with his arms. "I know. But you were sleeping and I can't find Mama anywhere I look."

"She's gone to the next town," I said immediately. "I need some things for the séance."

Byron's voice was small in my ear. "Doesn't it bother you? Them saying those things about us? About us . . . eating folks like we were savages?"

I rolled over within the circle of his arms until we were facing one another. "Have you ever eaten a man?" I asked him. "And before you answer, really think. You've eaten a lot of meals in your life, maybe thousands, and under some dodgy circumstances. Can you really say for absolute certainty that just a little bit, just a morsel of human meat has never, *ever* passed your lips?"

I watched his eyes get big.

"You would never know if you did," I teased. "We taste just like what we are. We taste like animal meat."

Of course, if Byron had eaten a human person, I wasn't the one who fed it to him, but he didn't seem to know that. The ghosts of a thousand roast dinners and cold meat lunches were moving over his pallid, horrified face. I almost laughed but managed to restrain myself.

"I will tell you a story," I said, "about before we met, when I was just a little girl in Sweden. One year, when I was eight years old, the winter came and did not end. Not in March or April or May. My father—my real father—was a farmer but he was not a good one. He was not lucky and he was not patient, and he was not good at reading the earth or the sky. You need all those things to be a farmer and sometimes, even with them, the earth finds a way to swallow you up.

"My father imagined that he would raise fruit trees and he sank everything we had, our money, our time, our manpower, into planting a great orchard that was supposed to make us rich. A heavy frost killed them all, root and branch. We had nothing left, except our debts.

"The man who ran the store let us buy on credit

until the snows made the usual trade routes impassible. He had to reserve his stock, first for the paying customers, then for his own small family. My father respected him for the choice. He said a man must look to his own before anything else.

"We ate the seed we'd reserved for the next year. We ate the goats we'd kept for milk and the old mare father used to pull the sledge. One very bad night, my mother boiled the laces from all our shoes, and we ate a tasteless, gelid soup made from the little scraps of leather.

"Marten was the hired man. Man, I say, though he was just fifteen. He had no mother nor father and he worked for us in exchange for a bed and meals. We could still provide the bed but it had been long since we could offer him a meal.

"A man—a father—must look to his own first. That's what my father believed, and so when the little food we had was portioned out, it was Marten who always got the least of it. At first, he did not complain because he knew his position in our house.

Then he did not complain because he was dying. We were all dying, but Marten was dying the fastest.

"It didn't look like he was shrinking—getting smaller, I mean. It was actually the opposite. It looked like Marten's bones were growing, swelling and swelling and pushing up through his skin in points and right-angles. It looked like something was being exposed, as when the tide retreats and the rocks rise out of the sea.

"He got these sores around his mouth, red craters that glistened with clear liquid. His lips were moving all the time, trembling. His eyes were always half-lidded but staring as though he were waiting for something we could not—or would not—see.

"Marten was the weakest, but none of us were strong. We did not work or play or read or sew. We only slept, nearly all hours of the day and night. Mother made an enormous bed for all of us on the floor in front of the fire—mother, father, my little sister Agneta and I. Even Marten, because he still had some small warmth to offer us. We would all pile upon one another, using our bodies as bulwarks against the cold.

"Inside our pitiable cave, the stink was incredible. It smelled like urine and like dirty mouths, dry and stale. But mostly we smelled like a wound after the rot has set in, when there is nothing left to do but amputate.

"My father was the strongest of us. It was he who went out to fetch wood for the fire and he who helped mother slowly, laboriously, squat over the chamber pot. And it was he who gave us life once more.

"Agneta asked weakly what he was doing as he disentangled Marten from our human knot, but Father said nothing. He picked up the starving boy, one arm under his shoulders, one under his knees. It was snowing hard and when Father took Marten outside, they vanished almost immediately into whiteness.

"When he came back, he was carrying something wrapped in tarpaulin and it was dripping dark fluid.

It smelled coppery and cold and made a bitter taste in the back of my mouth. I swallowed, only to discover that my mouth was flooded with saliva for the first time in days.

"I don't know if father thought it was indecent to cook up human meat with herbs and spices you'd use on venison or turkey, or if he was just too exhausted to make the effort, but he only put the cuts from the canvas into a pan and let them heat through on the fire. When my mother smelled the cooking meat, she started to moan.

"Father gave us each a portion of the meat and told us that it would make us strong again. He was right."

I stroked Byron's hair. Already the walnut dye was starting to fade and his own true yellow color was showing through at the top of his head.

"Never let them make you feel bad," I whispered to him, "for doing those things that you have to do." He had tucked his face into the gap between my chin and collarbone. I could not see his expression, so I found his jaw with my fingertips and forced his head upwards.

"We did what we needed to do and we are here now, alive. So we must have done something right." I gave his nose a flick and thereby drew a smile from him once again.

* * *

Nesbitt was building his home on a long protruding butte at the edge of town. The structure itself was an odd and imposing thing, built around an incredible central tower, still half-finished and wearing an awful hole where I suspected a clock face was meant to go.

He greeted me at the door when I arrived, shortly before dusk. Clearly, the man had either no staff or a very small one.

"Look at you!" he boomed in greeting. "Are you in mourning?"

I had chosen a small, dark bonnet with a veil that

covered my eyes and terminated just above my chin. It was black needle lace with an intricate pattern that largely hid my face from view. A more ideal piece of millenary for a séance, I could not imagine.

"The light," I told him, "bothers my eyes."

Inside, the house smelled of fresh-cut lumber and a bit like the joss sticks the Chinese burned to talk to their gods. There was a carpet in the long hall behind the door, but where it ended, the floor transformed into a mere framework of bracing boards.

"Walk along the beams," Nesbitt advised me.

He moved me along at a brisk pace, but I caught a glimpse of what was likely a sitting room, illuminated by the enormous hole in the wall where the clock face wasn't and a tightly curled staircase that led to the barest sketches of an upper floor.

The back parlor was the only entirely finished room that I could see so far. The floors there were smooth and perfect, overlaid with an intricate rug from parts unknown, the large windows thoughtfully covered with heavy curtains. There was even a full complement of furniture, including an enormous circular table with five chairs set around it. A parlor just for séances, and Royal Nesbitt had completed this before bothering to finish the roof.

Lucille sat before a small fireplace where only a little pile of coals was glowing, offering minimal heat and even less light. She turned slightly at our arrival but almost immediately pivoted back around.

"This is your room," Nesbitt told me warmly, resting a surprisingly heavy hand on my inert shoulder. "Or a room for someone like you. When I went looking for a place to build this house, I got an Apache medicine man to find the best spot for me."

Lucille leaned forward with a metal poker to push the coals into life.

I nodded deeply. "There is something here," I said, "something ancient and important."

"Goodness!" A figure rose from the darkest corner of the room, furthest from the door. "Is this the woman you told me about?"

The figure strode across the room and into the light, revealing himself to be a young man with a prodigious mustache and very well-groomed hair. "Why, you're just a bit of a thing!" he laughed, peering closely at my face, or what he could puzzle out of it below the veil.

When I said nothing to this, he jutted out his hand for shaking. "Pruitt—Hindley Pruitt. I run *The Creek Crier*."

I met his eyes through my veil. "I don't believe I know what that is."

He laughed again, though he sounded considerably less amused. "It's the newspaper of record for this town."

"Hindley is also a bit of an amateur investigator in the realm of spiritualism." Nesbitt's voice was very arch, and he looked at Pruitt over my head, the two of them sharing a great joke at my expense.

"Just a hobby really," Pruitt demurred. "I prefer to investigate real stories."

"Like that of the awful cannibal family in Kansas?" I did not entirely mean to say it; it flew from my mouth carelessly, like some stinging insect.

Pruitt's eyes gleamed. "So you *have* seen the paper!"

I decided right then that if the opportunity arose, I was going to kill this man.

"If you ask me," Nesbitt began, in the truest fashion of someone who had definitely *not* been asked, "I think they went mad out there on the prairie." He moved over to Lucille and touched her shoulder, turning her slightly so she was facing the rest of us. "Your people have some story like that, don't they? Some demon called the Wendigone?"

"*Wendigo*," Lucille corrected.

"Yes, of course. Sneaks in under men's skins and turns them wild, has them eating human flesh." He leaned close to her and bugged his eyes, holding his hand up like a claw.

"That is . . . not exactly right," Lucille said.

"I have heard of such things," I offered. "A tall,

thin, hungry thing that stalks the forests. A kind of demon, I thought."

"There are many stories," Lucille kept shifting slightly, as though she longed to turn back to the coals but Nesbitt's hand restrained her.

"It wasn't demons that killed all those poor folks out on the prairie," Pruitt offered. "Just ordinary men and women without conscience, without heart."

"Very astute." I brushed past him to examine the table. "Your medicine man," I turned to Nesbitt, "did he read the rest of the house?"

"Read?"

"Examine it spiritually. Determine where the weak places might be, where the spirits may congregate?" Nesbitt shook his head and I mirrored him dolefully. "I'm afraid I will have to postpone our sitting a bit. I must tour the house to make sure it is safe to contact the spirit realm here. If I did not do that, we could very well find ourselves opening a portal we could not close again."

Nesbitt's face was rapt, Pruitt looked as though he longed to laugh, and Lucille was stoic as always.

I was surprised, then, when she rose from her chair (sending Nesbitt's hand tumbling from her shoulder) and said, "I will take you."

• • •

The house was cold, the oncoming night air streaming in unchecked, and Lucille was hardly warmer. She led me through unfinished sitting rooms and guest rooms and even a barren little water closet with nary a word. She did not speak at all, in fact, until we climbed the twisting staircase to examine the empty cage of beams that would one day be Royal Nesbitt's office.

"Pruitt thinks you are a fraud," Lucille said as I peered out the square gap where a window would eventually go.

Inside the unfinished wall across from us, someone had safely nestled a modest cast-iron safe with modest wooden inlay. I tried not to stare at it. Instead, I turned my attention to Lucille's face. "What do you think?"

Lucille paused and chose her words carefully. "I think you aren't from Russia."

I smiled thinly. "And your mother was no Frenchwoman."

"My mother was Ojibwa and my father too," Lucille admitted. "No chiefs or princesses, just two people who made a child. It was Royal who contrived the other story."

I had presumed as much. A clever person would have selected a swarthier sort of foreigner, perhaps an Italian or a Spaniard, to square with Lucille's coloring.

"What happened to them?" For the first time, I lifted my veil from my face.

Lucille peered at me, looking for some sort of clue in my exposed eyes and mouth. "My father died before I was born. Someone told me years later that he had been shot by a white man, though I don't know why. I hardly suppose it matters. When I was four, I went to the Indian School."

"Your mother sent you?"

Lucille's face twisted. "I remember very little of that time in my life. Mostly, I remember my mother's hands. She had very long, strong fingers. I remember watching her rip the seam out of a shirt and how she plucked up the thread with her nails and tore it out with one quick, twisting motion." Her voice had gone distant and halting, like someone attempting to recount a strange dream.

"The school was operated by a Presbyterian minister and his wife," she continued in a blander, more practiced tone. "The minister's wife told me that my mother had died. Encephalitic flu. I do not know, however, if that actually happened. The minister's wife believed in telling children and Indians only those truths that would benefit them."

"Did you never try to find her again? Your mother, I mean."

Lucille smiled benevolently at me. "When I

was nine, Royal came to the school and selected me from amongst all the other girls. He sent me to school in England and in France and two months ago, when I turned seventeen, he retrieved me and we came here. I have had little time for investigations."

"And when did you have time to learn so much about Russians?"

"Your accent is terrible," she said flatly. "Royal doesn't notice because he wants you to be . . . magical, I suppose. Are you planning to rob him?"

"I should hope I won't have to."

Lucille looked less than satisfied with my answer. "I know I should feel loyal to him," she said. "He paid for my upbringing. Gave me everything I have."

But I don't remained unspoken, though the sentiment was clearly visible in her face.

I went back to the open window gap and hooked my hands around what would become the window-sill. I stared down at the grounds where Byron was hiding, dutifully awaiting my signal. That was loyalty, I thought—squatting in the cold for no reason other than that I had instructed him to.

"I bet it never snows here," I murmured.

"Where did you learn of the *wendigo?*" Lucille's footsteps were small and light but I could feel her draw closer to me.

"Michigan. It is a cold-weather monster, don't you think?"

"It's not a monster," Lucille said.

I turned to find her right behind me, leaning toward me like an eager conspirator. "What is it, then?" I smiled.

"It's . . . a story that we tell."

"So you don't believe in it?" I was teasing her now, like a girlhood friend, and for my efforts, I received the smallest of smiles.

"That's not what I said. Don't you know by now how a thing can be a story and be true as well?"

"How's that?"

"I think the *wendigo* is a way of talking about a

truth. I think that, when you take something as precious as another's life to satisfy your own hunger, to fill your own belly at their expense, I think something does change in you."

"You grow tall and starving and sprout long, sharp fangs?"

Her face grew suddenly very serious. "No. You do it again. And again and again, until it doesn't feed you anymore. But it will always feed you and you'll never stop hungering. That is why we have only one cure for the *wendigo*."

"And what is that?"

"Death," she said lightly, turning her face to look out the window with me. "I don't think it ever does," she added, almost offhandedly. "Snow, I mean. Not here in Nesbitt's Creek."

•   •   •

"Selfish," Mamma had called me, "wicked," and worse, "*disloyal*." She said that I had already abandoned them, as surely as if I had climbed aboard the train and whisked myself away.

"I looked upon you as my daughter," she said, "ever since you walked into my house!" But once again she had forgotten the work I did, how I waited and pried and learned how to cajole her before she gave me the smallest share of respect. Bodily children never did so much to earn their parents' consideration.

There was one way, however, in which she had certainly thought of me as a daughter— she had never imagined that I might harm her. If she had done, she would have told Fader and Byron immediately upon discovering the bag, or she might have taken it for herself and run. What she most certainly would not have done was confront me alone in our closed room, where there was a set of heavy andirons close at hand to brain her with.

She fought me hard but she was surprised, and because of that, I got the first strike. It's very hard to recover from a blow to the head, even for a large and hale woman. She tried to grab my arms but she was probably seeing double because her wild attempts to clasp my arms were well to the left of me. I skirted her easily, getting behind her and wrapping the sleeve of a discarded gown around her neck. I pulled it fast and, combined with the wound to her skull, it quickly rendered her slow and quiescent. And then, finally, she was very still indeed.

It was a sorry thing and not what I would have chosen for either of us, but I could not allow her to ruin our work in Nesbitt's Creek, not when it was so very close to being done. It takes a strong person to do the hard things that survival requires. I learned that when I was very young. The long winter of my childhood tempered me and showed me all that I could do if I had to.

My father cut himself one day when he went out to chop more wood for us, and the wound grew sweet and fetid until the poison seeped into his blood and he died. Mother and I struggled to push his corpse out of the cabin into the snow where his body would wait until spring. We did not even attempt to eat from his body because we knew better than to consume infected meat. After that Mother grew sicker and sicker and smaller and smaller until her head looked like a deeply grooved walnut and her hair came out in big white clumps.

When we woke up one morning and Mother would not move or speak, I remembered what my father had done for us with Marten. I knew nothing of butchery and little enough of cooking, but I managed because I had to. As for my little sister, she was already a wasted little creature, her huge skull balanced precipitously on her skeletal body. I remember, too, what my father has said about eating the meat and how one portion would make me strong. Surely two portions would make me twice as strong.

By the time that terrible winter ended, I was the only living thing in our cabin. And then even I was gone, off to the city where I would meet Fader and he would teach me nearly everything. Everything except for the most important thing, which I had just discovered for myself—how to always survive, no matter the cost.

9

Recompense

Emmelene Drake and Lawce Gibbon
Nesbitt's Creek, New Mexico
February, 1872

On the pretext of finding the outdoor water closet, I excused myself from Lucille and slipped down to the kitchen where I unlatched the back door for Byron.

"There are bedrooms on the top and bottom floor but not too much stuff moved in," I whispered. "Concentrate on the safe upstairs, first room on your right."

I took his hands, cold and half-balled into fists and gave them a warm squeeze. "I'll give you as much time as I can," I promised.

"I planted all the burners," he said, showing me

the empty innards of a gunnysack he had brought to carry the small fire-starting devices we had crafted together from rags and grease and hard, dense wood. I had wondered, seeing the soft stone of the house's exterior, whether it would take the flames but I knew that there was enough unfinished wooden architecture inside the place to bring it down. If we both did our jobs well, though, there would be no need for such theatrics. I kissed Byron's cheek. "Good boy," I said.

"I will require full dark, I'm afraid," I said, sweeping into the séance parlor and casting a baleful look at the coals in the fireplace. Nesbitt muffled the fire himself, shoving the coals deep into the back of the fireplace. Pruitt checked the heavy curtains on the windows before settling himself expectantly at the table.

The room was black, and we were all just a collection of shadows, moving into position around the table.

"Please," I said, sitting down, "link hands."

On my right was Lucille's hand, as small as my own and oddly cold. On my left was Pruitt's, long-fingered and warm.

"Why is it that the spirits seem always to love the dark?" Pruitt asked, in a voice presumably meant to sound just idly questioning. "All manner of mischief can be concealed in the low light, after all. Why don't they show themselves clearly?"

"We shall make our own light, Mr. Pruitt. And, I assure you, you shall see everything clearly."

"You know, I have read of mediums who perform in the all-together. Just in the interests of demonstrating that they are not smuggling tricks in their skirts."

"That would be unnecessary." I imagined his face, somehow both smug and leering at the same time. "And certainly not definitive, for you must surely know that God himself made plenty a *smuggling place* on the human body as well."

Pruitt snorted.

Across from me, Royal Nesbitt fidgeted excitedly

in his seat. "If I may ask, Madame, who are your controls?"

He wanted to know which individual spirit— usually a particularly strong and wise one (often a red Indian or an ancient Egyptian princess)—would be inhabiting my body and guiding the séance.

Unfortunately, I was going to have to disappoint him. "Sir, I control myself. At all times."

•   •   •

"No one like that is staying in this hotel," the attendant said, shaking his head in mock disapproval. "And, I can assure you, we would not court that sort of clientele."

"You dumb fuck," Charlie said and, for once, I was thankful that I had my brother along on an errand. "They wouldn't come in here dripping gore and booking under the name Drake. They're in hiding! Who has booked a room in the last two weeks?"

The attendant pursed his lips and blew out a gust of air as though we'd asked him to do a particularly difficult cipher. "Oh, lots of folks. Some men looking to prospect out here—we have a very rich silver vein, you know—"

"Any women?" Charlie snapped.

"Well, there's Mrs. Inez Gordon and her daughters, Joan and Marie and Sophie and Eleanor . . . " He ticked each name off on his fingers and I wondered if he was being deliberately obtuse. "And there are the old sisters Mrs. Barrow and Mrs. Frederickson. Oh! And of course there is Madame Olginskaya."

"Who is that?" Charlie leaned across the desk, taking a surreptitious glance at the reservation book as he did so.

"She's a very celebrated medium," the attendant sounded shocked that Charlie could be ignorant of her exploits. "She has performed many impressive feats right here in this very hotel."

"The big suite down the hall," Charlie said. I

gestured toward the rest of the men waiting in the lobby and we all rushed for the doorway.

As soon as he saw what we were doing, the attendant ran around the counter and tried to block our passage. "You can't just burst into a guest's room!"

The sheriff elbowed him aside hard and exposed his sidearm. "Go back to your desk," he said, all the weariness of the many miles from Madalane to Nesbitt's Creek in his voice. The attendant must not have been a true idiot after all because he turned around abruptly and went back to his post.

We found the door shut and locked, and no one answered when Pap knocked. Both Harris and Charlie immediately tried to break the door down. They mostly crowded each other out, but they did manage to tilt the door inwards until we could get a glimpse of the room inside. There were no flickers of movement so far as I could tell and no sign that anyone was inside to react to our messy fumblings.

Harris put his shoulder to the door once again, this time stumbling through it entirely while the jagged pieces left clinging to the hinges rebounded off the wall noisily. As I had suspected, there was no sign of anyone in the large and luxurious suite, which could not have presented more a contrast with the Drakes' cramped cabin in Kansas.

There was one way, however, in which the two places were just alike. Pap was the first to notice it, his nose twitching in the air like a dog's. He looked at Charlie who nodded and by now even I had realized what they were smelling. It was the same smell that accompanied that awful hide under the Drakes' bed and the exact stink that had risen out of the doctor's homely little grave: the smell of something dead, getting deader.

Wordlessly, we moved around the room, searching for the source of the awful stench. Finally, we converged upon a large steamer trunk, set upon its side as if to serve as a wardrobe. It was not locked, so when Charlie pulled the lid open, the body inside fell halfway out immediately, her lower extremities still jammed in the confines of the trunk.

Charlie made an involuntary noise and turned his face away, burying his nose in his elbow to block the stink. The woman in the wardrobe—it was immediately clear that it was a woman from her dress and her long, unbound gray hair—was "fresh" and the smell was even more powerful than it had been back at the Drake homestead.

Pap toed the trunk open further until the body fell entirely to the floor, still curled into the shape of the trunk. She landed with her face staring upwards and it was a horrible thing indeed. There was blood in clotted streams on her forehead, over her nose and mouth, crusted in her hair, and her face was an awful bruised purple-black color. Her eyes were open and blind, protruding from her skull.

"Strangled," Pap said, pointing to a length of something like silk that I had not even noticed, so deeply was it embedded in the skin of her throat.

"Looks like old Mrs. Drake," the sheriff said, though how he could see anything familiar in that agonized, bloated visage, I did not know.

"Damn it all, I had a key," the attendant said sourly, pushing through the crowd of us until he reached the sheriff. "You gonna pay for this?" he demanded.

"You aware you had a murder in your hotel?" the sheriff countered, pointing toward the body on the floor.

The attendant turned to look at it, and my estimation of his fortitude went up by several notches when he barely flinched. "Shit," he said.

"The young woman who traveled with her, the Madame Olga-something, where is she?" Charlie asked.

The attendant shook his head. "I don't ask them where they're going."

From behind us, we heard the howl of metal hinges. A man stood—leaned, really—in the shattered remnants of the door and tossed it idly back and forth between his hands. His long shaggy mane had been clipped off around his head and his beard was gone, but we all recognized Old Man Drake when we saw him.

"I heard fighting," he slurred.

"Where is your daughter?" Charlie asked him and he laughed.

"No daughter," he said, his voice halting and thick. "Never had one."

"Where is she?"

Mr. Drake pointed out the window in a vaguely easterly direction. "Big house," he said. "*Viktig* man. Where else can she be?"

. . .

Phosphorescent paint was an incredible substance which I had learned about from an amateur chemist in Chicago. When properly activated, it glowed an eerie greenish-white, even in the lowest of lights. While Byron had patiently torn rags and soaked them in lamp oil, I had been filling large, empty capsules with portions of the thick liquid. I had then attached the capsules to the soft interior of my elbows in such a position that, with only a small compression by my arm muscles, I might rupture the capsules and send the paint spilling forth.

"There is someone with us," I said, before flexing my inner arm until I felt a small burst and a trickle of wetness. The paint flowed down my forearm in rivulets, looking something like veins filled with glowing blood. I heard a small gasp from Mr. Pruitt as he noticed my new supernatural affliction.

"This person is strong and . . . angry . . . " There was a certain delight to performing that I had nearly forgotten. I could hear how their breathing had slowed and tensed. I could not see their eyes, but I knew that they were fixed upon me and my spectral wounds.

"A male presence," I said. "This is his place. This *was* his place." I squeezed the hands on either side of me as though in a spasm. "Royal Nesbitt, you took it from him. Something is coming through." I twisted and writhed in my seat as though rocked by unearthly forces. I also took the opportunity to slip my hand from Pruitt's slackened grasp and, delicately and very quickly, transfer Lucille's hand from my own to Pruitt's.

For half a breath, I waited to see if either of them would notice the switch or, more importantly, if they would make an objection but both parties remained silent. With my hands free, I rolled up my sleeves and wiped the remaining paint from my skin with the underside of my skirt. It was very easy then to produce my next prop, a long slender feather, also strategically painted with luminescent liquid. I drew it up from my collar, carefully shielding the glow with my hand until I reached my mouth, where I pretended to retch, making awful gagging sounds as I "produced" the ethereal object.

"Do you recognize this, Royal Nesbitt?" I intoned.

"Is it . . . from a war bonnet?" Nesbitt wondered eagerly. "Is the spirit an Indian brave?"

"He claims you owe him a debt, and if you do not repay it, all of your endeavors will sour and your rich veins of silver will dry up to nothingness."

Nesbitt leaned forward until I could see the contours of his pudgy face in the greenish glow of the feather. "How do I repay him?" he asked.

"First—" I said, but I was destined never to complete my thought.

The first sound—a low thump—from high above us might have been confused for an unfinished house moaning in the wind, or even for the machinations of the spirits. The second sound, however, was unmistakable: the strike of metal upon metal. A vision came to me, though an entirely natural one: Overwhelmed with the task of opening the safe, Byron was battering it with his tools, though he knew better. How many times had I told him to be quiet, to be gentle?

"Don't break the circle!" I cried as Nesbitt got to his feet.

"That came from my office!" he insisted.

"It may be a manifestation."

"May?" Pruitt asked, also rising from the table. If I allowed them to leave this room, everything we worked for would be lost.

"Mr. Nesbitt," I said calmly, "I have a firearm on your lady." It was not a lie. For this very purpose I had purchased (via Byron) an old Colt Walker revolver and carried it into Nesbitt's home in a pouch sewn into the lining of my inner skirt. I removed it now and pressed it into Lucille's side so she could attest to the weapon's reality.

For a moment, no one moved, and I was afraid that I had overestimated Nesbitt's fondness for his "ward." I was relieved, then, when he set down beside me, his breathing loud and ragged.

"You as well, Mr. Pruitt," I said to the newspaperman who was still standing. He stalked over to Nesbitt's vacated seat and planted himself there.

I stood up, pulling Lucille up with me and went to the window, where I threw open the window shades and let in the delicate moonlight until I could see the room clearly. Nesbitt was looking from Lucille back to me and Pruitt was looking at the gun. We all heard the clatter of Byron's boots on the staircase.

He knocked on the door and even the rap of his knuckles sounded sheepish. "You can come in, Byron," I snapped. Lucille flinched as though I had struck her.

Byron crept in, both hands on the edge of the door like a nervous child. "I suppose you all heard that?" he said dispiritedly, seeing the gun and the stiff way we all peered at one another. "I couldn't get the safe," he told me unnecessarily.

"It's all right, Byron. I'll fix it. But you go now and you light the matches. I'll be along in a little while."

He left the door open and I watched as he vanished down the long, unfinished hallway. I should have been paying more attention because that was when Pruitt launched himself out of his seat, grabbing me about the waist and forcing me to the floor. I kicked wildly underneath him, but he was much taller than I and considerably heavier. My only advantage was the grip I still held on the gun. I was trying to maneuver it into position when there came a long, low whistle through the air and Pruitt slumped against me, suddenly dead weight.

I pushed him off myself and jumped to my feet, my gun held out at no one in particular. I was surprised to see Lucille standing there, the fireplace poker in her hands and still raised as if to administer another blow. If I was surprised, Royal Nesbitt was shocked.

"Lucille!" he said, "what the hell are you doing?"

"My name is not Lucille," she snapped, regripping the poker with conviction. "My mother named me June; the Indian school even called me that. Why did you think you could change it?"

Nesbitt sputtered something wordless and mystified while I got my bearings. I lowered the gun, though only slightly, and kept it generally pointed in Nesbitt's direction. "So you are working with this confidence trickster?" he demanded.

"I wasn't," the erstwhile Lucille said, "but all I want to do is leave this place and she can help me do that." She turned to me and, for the first time, there was something doubtful and hesitant in her aspect. "Can't you?" she asked, in a slightly softer voice.

"Sure I can. I *will*."

"She's a thief," Nesbitt broke in. "A degenerate."

Lucille half-stepped forward and lowered the poker slightly, as though she were about to argue with Nesbitt. She did not get the chance, however, because Pruitt stirred then, still lying on the intricate, undoubtedly imported carpet. I stretched out my right hand and fired a bullet into the top of his skull.

He twitched once when the bullet entered his brain and then did not move again.

Nesbitt gasped. Lucille made no sound, but when she looked at me next, her eyes had gotten huge. It was the expression of one who has realized too late that they have gambled everything they have upon the wrong horse.

"Get up," I said to Nesbitt, "and take me to the safe. Both of you."

•   •   •

We saw the house long before we arrived. We saw the flames.

"Shit!" Charlie leapt from the buggy before the horses had even halted in front of the place. Smoke was curling out of the many openings in the edifice, and there were at least four different places where fires were actively burning.

"Set up a bucket chain!" I shouted to Pap and the others. "Bring water!"

Suddenly, Charlie set off at a dead run, but not toward the house itself. Instead, he ran toward an empty stretch of desert to the left of the mansion. I squinted until I saw a dark figure running through the scrubland with Charlie close behind him. I darted off into the dark toward the two of them.

The running figure was apparently not particularly dexterous, however, because he tripped on something in the earth and went down hard. Charlie pulled up short behind him and stomped on the figure's back.

I heard a sharp cry as I approached, and in the

moonlight, Charlie and I could both see that it was Byron Drake he had caught underneath his boot.

"I don't have anything," he said, his face half-muffled by the dirt.

Charlie pulled him to his feet violently. "What are you doing out here?"

"Setting the fire."

"Why?" I could not help but ask, though I realized as I said it that it was perhaps the least pressing of the questions to be asked at that moment.

"Because Em told me to."

"But why did she tell you—"

"Why are you wasting your time with a halfwit?" Charlie asked at the same time Byron answered, "To get rid of the bodies."

Emmelene Drake was planning another disappearing act. She was going to take everything of value in that house and then melt into the desert the same way the whole family had vanished out of Madalane. *She is the smart one*, Katie had said.

"Is she still inside?" Charlie grabbed Byron's

chin and forced the young man to look directly at him. There was no fear in Byron's face, just that same dull placidity, like a particularly fat and incurious cow.

"Yep," said Byron. "She won't leave until the work is done. She never does."

And if we did not catch her now—or else ensure that she died in the conflagration—then she would go on to do her work again someplace else, someplace we did not know and could not discover.

Behind us, we heard the shouts of the men as they organized into bucket lines and, even louder than that, the unholy crackle of the fire as it grew, feeding itself on Royal Nesbitt's unfinished palace.

10

Misfire

Lawce Gibbon and Emmelene Drake
Nesbitt's Creek, New Mexico Territory
February, 1872

Charlie stopped only to hand Byron off to the sheriff before charging back toward the house. I made to go after him when, to my great surprise, Pap caught my shirtsleeve.

"Lawce," he said, "don't go in there."

"Emmelene Drake is in there and some other folks who don't deserve to die burning."

"It's going up," Pap insisted. "There isn't enough water and there isn't enough time. You go in there, you may well die."

Ahead of us, at the fiery doorway of the house, I could see Charlie's outline. He had paused momentarily to watch us. I had a vision then, a perfect image of Charlie emerging from a wall of flames with Emmelene Drake by the hair, while with his other hand he ushered a small group of shivering innocents to freedom. Even though it only existed in my mind, the vision churned something awful in my stomach, the bitterest kind of jealously. Whether it was glory or death in that house, I could not allow Charlie to have it all for himself.

"Sorry," I told Pap before breaking from his grasp and rushing for the front door—and for Charlie.

The house was silver-blue with smoke, but there were no active flames that I could see and the temperature was not oppressive. Charlie and I flipped the edges of our shirts up over our noses and mouths as we moved along the hallway, pushing aside doors and calling out for anyone who might be alive and listening.

Most of the rooms were empty, but one toward the back of the house contained a sprawled figure lying very still on the floor. Charlie ran to him and tried to lift him up shouting "Jesus Christ!" when his hands came away bloody.

We ran back to the hallway and it seemed to me that the fire itself was getting louder, the crackles and pops sharper and more intimate. Distantly, we heard the sounds of boots scuffling upstairs and a number of loud pops. Perhaps it was the crackling of the fire, but I believed it to be gunshots, especially considering the heavy thump that followed them. The sound of a body hitting the floor.

· · ·

"Open it," I said, resting the barrel of my gun lightly on the back of Nesbitt's neck.

"There's nothing in it." Nesbitt fumbled with a small metal key that he kept on his waistcoat, his fingers nearly pruned with his own sweat. "I don't keep any money here."

"Shut the fuck up," I said, certain that it was a

sentiment that Royal Nesbitt had not heard nearly often enough in his life.

Beside him, Lucille had gone blank faced again, but I knew that behind her careful glamour of nothingness, her mind was whirring away.

Nesbitt swung the safe open finally to reveal a sad little pile of paperwork and a white gleam of some sort of jewel. "See?" he said. "Was this worth your time?"

"Hand it to me," I told Lucille, who promptly scooped up the papers and pressed them into my waiting hand. I glanced through them quickly, gun still on Nesbitt and could not keep myself from grinning. Not only did the stack contain several deeds to land in and around Nesbitt's Creek, it also had a veritable cache of documentation for Miss Lucille Bonheur, soon-to-be bride of Mr. Royal Nesbitt.

The glinting jewel turned out to be a truly gaudy yellow diamond in a silver band. I slipped it on my own ring finger and found it an excellent fit.

"That was to be yours," Nesbitt told Lucille

dispiritedly but she gazed not upon her lost ring. She was looking at my face, my smile.

"Neither of us is leaving this place alive, are we?" she asked softly.

"Sorry, Mademoiselle," I said and I meant it truly. "But only one Lucille Bonheur can leave this house tonight."

Nesbitt must have supposed that I was distracted or that I was stupid enough to fall for the same trick twice in less than an hour, because he tried to swing at me while I talked to Lucille. I turned on my heel and fired three shots into him in short succession. The first struck him in his outstretched hand and fist, the second hit him somewhere in his middle, and the third got him right in the throat.

He fell to the ground with considerably more scrabbling and writhing than Mr. Pruitt. Lucille squeezed her eyes closed at the reports of the revolver, but otherwise had no reaction. On the floor between us, Nesbitt gurgled, blood puddling up in his mouth.

"You don't have to," Lucille said, over the sounds of her paramour struggling for his last breath. "I told you, all I want is to leave this place. You can go be Lucille. I never wanted to be her anyway."

I looked at her with genuine pity. What an awful thing it was, not to be able to save oneself. Then I pointed the Colt Walker at her and fired.

I registered the pain first, a searing heat in my right hand. When I looked down at the gun, I saw not a weapon but a ruined piece of blown-out metal, a crater where the cylinder should have been.

I struggled to hold onto the gun, but I could not force my fingers to obey the demands of my brain. The revolver hit the floor with a thunk and I lifted my damaged hand. My skin was streaked with black powder and red blood. My first two fingers were twisted into improbable shapes. The pain was incredible but very distant, as though it had happened to someone I once knew intimately, or myself a long time ago.

Byron. That goddamned idiot. The Colt was old

and fussy, the best that we could afford. How often had I told him to lard up the cylinders so the black powder didn't burst all the chambers at once? And how many times had my admonitions slipped right out of his empty fucking head?

The explosion of the gun had rendered us both momentarily frozen, but Lucille recovered first, rushing at me and grabbing for the papers in my left fist. I laughed as I raised my elbow to collide with her face. She attacked my wounded hand viciously, twisting it and crushing it in her own fist.

"You did nothing to earn that!" she shrieked at me, tearing at the paperwork with her fingernails. I laughed again because she didn't know anything, that Miss Lucille: no one earned anything. You got what you could take and you have what you can keep.

I brought my knee up hard into her stomach and she fell back, the air knocked from her chest. I turned and ran for the staircase, but I didn't get more than three paces before she crashed into the back of me and sent the both of us sliding out onto one of the office's support beams, which moaned ominously under our weight.

She grabbed my left wrist and beat my hand against the beam, trying to force me to release to paperwork.

"The paperwork doesn't matter," I shouted at her. "You don't think I can be you? You're not a person, just a story that a rich man tells."

She coughed even as she pressed relentlessly into my struggling torso.

Below, gray smoke hissed through the gaps in the boards. "We are going to die here if we stay."

Lucille stopped. She looked at me like a dreamer arising from a daze. Had she forgotten where she was? Had she forgotten the flames? She opened her mouth to speak but, just then, there was a great and awful cracking, like a giant's bone snapping.

. . .

I got to the staircase just two steps or so ahead of Charlie. Through the unfinished support beams of the walls upstairs, I could make out two figures grappling violently with one another. I heard a woman scream, though I was not so familiar with Emmelene Drake that I could say it was her. Those sounds, however, were almost obliterated by a great cracking as the staircase below me crumpled into two distinct halves. For a wild moment, my right foot hung freely over an unknown expanse before I pulled myself up onto the next stair.

Below me on the lower half of the staircase, Charlie had crumpled along with the fire-damaged wood. He lay in a heap, fresh-cut boards scattered below him like a hard and awful bed. I stared at him, my knuckles white on the banister. I don't know if I wanted Charlie to move, to sit up, call to me and reassure me that he was alive and unhurt, or to simply lie there, still and silent, requiring nothing of me.

My mind returned again to that fleeting vision

I'd had of Charlie emerging triumphant from the flames. Only, this time, it was me pulling Emmelene Drake along like a sack of laundry, me guiding the wealthy man and his wife to safety. I could do it, I thought. There was time yet to scramble up the stairs where I could surprise Emmelene and force her out of the house.

But there was not time to do that and to remove Charlie as well.

Charlie, the unwanted appendix on my family, who would slice up my fortune and my livelihood; our father's legacy. Brutish Charlie, crude Charlie, handsome Charlie whom nearly everyone preferred. He could die here, he could even die a hero of sorts, and I could be a hero as well. The man who tried to save him and failed. I thought of Harris and his belief that taking part in the hunting party would wash away his own sins and absolve him of suspicion. He was probably right.

And then, for no reason at all, I thought of Katie Conkle and the way she had screamed at the half-hanged man out on the Drake homestead. The shine she had taken to me for intervening on the night of the chivaree. It seemed to me that if I could get a woman like Katie to look kindly upon me, then perhaps it would be worth a halved inheritance. Perhaps it was a wealth of its own.

I leapt down from the staircase, landing next to Charlie who was coughing from the smoke. Every time he drew breath, he winced. "My ribs," he panted. Up close, I could also see a long, thin splinter of wood sticking out of the meat of his right thigh.

"Here," I said, reaching down and encircling his waist with my arms. "Hold on to me."

*　*　*

Together, we were still and silent. It seemed that the whole world was swaying underneath us. Something had come unmoored beneath the office floor, and we wobbled delicately back and forth.

"You should have shot me first," Lucille whispered.

"Yep," I agreed. The world always makes us pay for every little kindness.

The new wood and whatever scented herbs Nesbitt had kept in the place actually created an odd, intoxicating scent as they burned all around us. When I looked over at Lucille, her face was oddly tranquil. "I'm not afraid," she said, as though she could read my mind. "I have never been afraid of dying here, only of living here."

I did not say anything to this and the floor moved again. In the space of a breath, the whole world descended, and we fell along with it.

* * *

I supported Charlie on my shoulder, his injured leg cocked in front of him. He hopped awkwardly out into the bitter night, grunting with pain every time he jostled himself. "Slow down," I told him, but he would not. "The whole place is going," he said, as we reached the threshold of the house. He was right. Later, Pap would tell me how, almost the moment we cleared the landing, the upper floor of the mansion collapsed in upon itself and sank into the lower floor, creating a kind of burn pit that would rage on until long after sunrise.

But that was later. When Charlie and I left the burning house, neither of us looked back. We moved forward, doggedly and painfully, until we reached Pap and the sheriff and the buggy. Pap helped me lift up Charlie, and we situated him in the back of the gig, keeping his leg raised. We didn't dare remove the splinter, lest he start gushing blood, and he refused to let us look at his ribs.

"Don't fuss," he said, lying back and closing his eyes.

So we didn't. Instead, we watched the mansion burn. "I put men all around the house," the sheriff said. "We'll see her if she tries to run."

I thought about the scream and scuffles I heard

just above us on the stairs. Emmelene was definitely in the house right before the collapse, and there was no way she was getting out of that alive.

"She won't run," I said.

I was surprised when Pap draped his arm over my shoulders, and I surprised him, I'm sure, when I leaned against him in return. We stood there for a long time, watching the flames rage down into charcoal and dust.

Epilogue

The porter was very glad to see the young woman with just the valise. It seemed that every year the wardrobe trunks grew larger, more elaborate, and inevitably heavier.

He offered to load the valise for her, but she shook her head politely. The day was warm but she wore a heavy black veil that a widow might sport, as well as long gloves, also black. When she adjusted her grip on the valise's handle, her hands moved oddly, as though the fingers there did not have full motion and remained instead locked in a claw shape.

"Thank you," she murmured to him as he helped

her aboard the train (he held her elbow and her entire arm shook in his grasp). Up close, he could see snatches of her face through the gaps in the lace pattern. It looked as though she had been disfigured in some way, burnt horribly, it seemed. Her right eye appeared to be entirely sightless, white as a billiard ball, and the lower lid pulled down grotesquely, like warm taffy.

He tried not to shudder as he handed her onto the train.

He watched through the train's windows as she made her way at a painfully slow clip down the aisle and settled herself in the window. She stared out of the glass but not at the station itself, seemingly at something beyond its walls. The train was headed west and the porter wondered where she was going. To a sick relative, perhaps? Or a very disappointed man? Probably she was going west for the same reason most other folks did—to disappear.

AUTHOR'S NOTE

By 1873, the people of Labette County, Kansas knew that something was seriously wrong.

Life was hard in southeastern Kansas. Labette and the areas around it were populated with homesteaders and other hardy folks willing to eke out an existence on what had been, until just a few years before, Osage Indian territory. Labette County was also located just off a popular trail leading further west, making it a good spot for travelers to rest or restock.

Some of these travelers would perish, of course, done in by the privations of the long journey west or accidents or encounters with vandals. Even by those standards, though, Labette County was dangerous. From 1871 to 1873, a number of corpses showed up on various local homesteads. These men had died violently, throats cut, skulls caved in. But it was the other people—those who passed through Labette and then seemed to vanish off the face of the earth—that were the real problem. By 1873, the part of the Great Osage Trail that passed through this area of Kansas had a bad reputation as a good place to go missing.

The people of Labette County and the surrounding area considered any number of theories to explain the disappearances, driving out suspected thieves and vandals to no effect. It was the deaths of the moderately wealthy George Newton Longcor and his tenacious neighbor Dr. William Henry York who finally exposed the predators hiding amongst the simple frontier folk.

Longcor went missing like so many others had on the Osage Trail but his case was different in one major respect: when he vanished, his neighbor, Dr. York, launched a full investigation. He personally set out from Independence, Kansas (where Longcor had also lived) and conducted interviews with every homesteader he could find along the way.

Eventually, Dr. York made his way to a modest inn run by a family of German immigrants, the Benders. They were well known in and around Labette County for their inn but mostly for their daughter, the charming and attractive Miss Kate Bender. In addition to operating an inn and general store with her family, she also billed herself as a healer and traveled around the Midwest, giving lectures about spiritualism.

Aside from Kate, however, the Benders were not very engaged with their community. Ma and Pa Bender spoke little English, instead relying upon Kate and her brother John to interpret for them. John, like Kate, was good-looking and sociable, albeit allegedly somewhat "simple." Although hardly universally adored (Ma Bender had a reputation as a "she-devil" due to a number of dust-ups with the neighbors, and not everyone approved of Kate Bender's table-rapping, not to mention her advocacy of free love) the Benders were accepted in Labette County as just another family of immigrants trying to make their way on the prairie.

Things changed, however, when Dr. York failed to return from his trip to the Bender inn and general store. Soon, his politically powerful brothers (including a colonel and a senator) had mounted a full expedition, some fifty men strong, to find out what had happened to poor, inquisitive Dr. York.

Upon reaching the Bender homestead, Dr. York's brother Colonel York was almost immediately convinced that the family had something to do with his brother's disappearance. The Benders were cagey and combative. At one point, Ma Bender cursed Colonel York and his men and kicked them out, revealing for the first time that she was actually fully fluent in English.

Now that the harsh light of suspicion was

turned on the Bender family, people began to emerge from the woodwork, telling unsettling tales of being threatened with knives, of Pa Bender and John hiding behind a curtain in the inn, apparently planning to spring forth and attack travelers. The people of Labette County were now certain that they had found the cause of all those missing people, the source of all those mutilated corpses, but they wanted to act within the bounds of the law. So the town fathers agreed to wait and secure search warrants for the Benders' homestead.

Fortune smiled upon the Bender family, though, and a powerful late winter storm swept over Labette County, slowing progress on everything, search warrants included. By the time the weather had cleared, travelers were reporting that the Bender homestead appeared abandoned and the family long gone.

When locals searched the inn and surrounding property, they found horrible confirmation of all their fears. There were more than a dozen bodies buried in shallow graves all over the Bender property. The bodies of Dr. York, his neighbor George Longcor and, most distressingly, Longcor's eighteen-month-old daughter were amongst them.

Searchers also found a trap door leading into a dirt cellar where the floor was so completely saturated with blood and gore that the entire room stank of decomposition. The family's M.O. quickly became clear. One of the Bender men would hide behind a curtain used to divide the cabin into a general store and a private living space, and a guest would be seated at the dinner table in front of the curtain. When the guests were distracted with a meal, one of the Benders would emerge from behind the curtain and use a hammer to bludgeon them.

The Benders had split up, taking trains to Texas and Missouri. After that, their trails grew muddy. It was eventually determined, however, that almost nothing the Benders claimed about themselves had been true. Ma and Pa Bender were not married. Ma Bender was not even German. Kate might have been Ma Bender's daughter but she definitely wasn't

Pa's, and John was probably an unrelated German man named John Gebhardt. Some in Kansas even claimed that, instead of brother and sister, Kate and John were actually husband and wife. None of them was actually named Bender.

The story of the Bloody Benders was huge news (photographs from the homestead were published in national newspapers, some of the first mainstream "crime scene photos"), and people all over the country reported sightings of Ma and Kate, Kate and John, or Pa Bender all by his lonesome. Law enforcement all over the country searched for the murderous foursome, but though several people claimed to have caught and summarily executed the Benders, no one could provide proof of their whereabouts.

Out in the wild, far from the established cities of the east, frontier communities demanded a certain degree of interdependence and cooperation if they were going to survive. The crimes of the Bender family were horrifying, not only because of their inherent depravity and violence, but also because they cast a shadow over that communal interdependence. A homesteader still needed to trust his neighbor, but now he could never do so without remembering the Benders and what had happened to those who had put their faith in the hands of a family they believed to be much like their own.